UNSOLVED!

Famous
Real-Life
Mysteries

UNSOLVED!

Famous Real-Life Mysteries

George Sullivan

SCHOLASTIC INC.
New York Toronto London Auckland Sydney

ISBN 0-590-42990-6

12 11   3 4 5 6 7 8/0

Printed in the U.S.A.   01

First Scholastic printing, January 1992

Contents

UNSOLVED!

Famous
Real-Life
Mysteries

Introduction

Everyone loves a mystery. There's real delight to be found in a story that can't be fully understood, a story you can puzzle over but never really solve.

Take the case of Isidor Fink, who was killed in his tiny laundry in New York City in March 1929. A woman in the apartment next door heard shots and then something heavy, like a body, thud to the floor. She called the police, who found the door bolted and the windows locked.

The police got into the laundry by lifting a small boy up to the transom, which he found locked. The boy smashed the glass, climbed inside, and unlocked the door. Fink, with two bullet holes in his chest and one in his wrist, was dead.

At first, the police thought it was suicide. But where was the gun? They tore the room apart but could find no weapon.

The police then decided it was a case of murder. But how did the gunman get into the room? And what was the motive? Money in the cash register had not been taken, and cash was found in Fink's trouser pocket.

A squad of handpicked detectives was assigned to the case. But they were baffled by it. No solution was ever found.

Mysteries such as that surrounding the death of Isidor Fink are the subject of this book. They are happenings of several different types for which no answer or explanation has been found.

Some of the cases are unsolved in the strictest meaning of the word. The case involving the San Francisco mass killer known as Zodiac is one example. It's been designated as "unsolved" by the San Francisco Police Department. New York City police also have a series of unsolved Zodiac killings on their hands.

In other cases, however, there is no question who did it. Yet there remain lingering doubts as to some of the circumstances of the case. The assassination in 1968 of Senator Robert F. Kennedy, brother of President John F. Kennedy, is an example. Robert Kennedy's assassin was tried, convicted, and is serving time in a California prison. But there is a good deal of evidence to lead experts to believe another gunman was involved. The murder of Robert Kennedy has only partially been solved.

Not every case presented in this book involves criminal activity. When two huge passenger airliners collided in the sky over the Grand Canyon in 1956, no law was broken. But that has not lessened the mysterious aspects of what happened to the aircraft and their crew members in the final moments before the planes struck one another.

As these paragraphs suggest, this book is a bit different from most. You get a chance to make up your own mind as to what happened; you're a participant.

But no matter how smart you might be, the best you'll be able to do is develop a theory. There's no explanation as to what really happened. Until new witnesses come forward or new facts are unearthed, no real solution is possible. These cases are unsolved!

Death of a Bully

Skidmore is a small farm town in the northwest corner of Missouri, about one hundred miles due north of Kansas City. It has 440 people, a filling station, bank, grocery store, tavern, grain elevator, and a blacktop main street. Beyond the town are rolling meadows, silos, and windmills.

Skidmore used to have a town bully — a big, burly, 47-year-old man, 5 feet 10, 265 pounds, with massive arms and bushy eyebrows and sideburns. Everyone in Skidmore was scared to death of him. His name was Kenneth Rex McElroy, but everyone called him Ken Rex.

Then one hot, steamy July morning in 1981, Ken Rex was shot to death while sitting in his pickup truck on Skidmore's main street. There were anywhere from twenty to sixty witnesses. But no one would admit seeing anything. The case remains unsolved.

"I'm sure they know who did it," Sheriff's Deputy David Owens said after the shooting, "but they won't say much. I tell you — it's been a tough row to hoe."

"Fact is," said a businessman in Maryville, a town about twelve miles to the east, "a lot of them think a lot higher of whoever pulled the trigger than of Mr. McElroy."

Ken Rex was the twelfth of thirteen children born to a poor farm family. Never a good student, he dropped out of school after the fifth grade. He never could read or write.

As far as anyone knows, Ken Rex never worked at a steady job. He earned money by leasing land around the farm where he worked. He also raised and trained coon dogs (which can be any breed of dog taught to hunt raccoons). Ken Rex had, in fact, an excellent reputation as a dog trainer.

Ken Rex almost always carried a thick wad of bills, but most people believed his money didn't come from leasing land or raising coon dogs. He was suspected of rustling hogs and cattle from his neighbors.

In 1980, Nodaway County, the county in which Skidmore is located, led the state of Missouri in stolen livestock. It had six times as many thefts as nearby counties. Ranchers who were aware of that fact were also aware that Ken Rex always had plenty of money.

He paid for his pickups in cash. He paid his lawyer in cash. He once tossed $8,000 on the bar at the D&G Tavern in Skidmore and told the bartender, "If that ain't enough, I've got a suitcase full at home."

Ken Rex had a well-deserved reputation as a brawler and a bully. He struck fear in people by stalking them, glaring at them in silence, staring them down. He carried a gun that he was quick to flash. It made people shudder, for he was known to have used it on occasion.

When Ken Rex came roaring into town in his battered Chevy pickup with its big mud flaps and gun rack on the roof, everyone got out of sight. It wasn't so much that they feared for their lives. They were worried they might see McElroy do something unlawful and they would be called upon to testify to it later.

"I think that he simply wanted to be big and important and have people afraid of him as he walked down the street," said one farmer. "Well, he got that. They were."

Farmer Romaine Henry once tried to chase Ken Rex off of his land. Ken Rex shot Henry in the belly with a charge of buckshot.

After Ken Rex was arrested and brought to trial, his lawyer got a couple of witnesses to swear that Ken Rex was with them at the time of the shooting. Ken Rex was acquitted.

In another shooting, charges against Ken Rex were dropped because nobody would testify against him.

In June 1980, Ken Rex was arrested again, this time for shooting Ernest Bowencamp, Skidmore's seventy-two-year-old grocer. The trouble began when a clerk in Bowencamp's store asked Ken Rex's eight-year-old daughter, Tonia, to return a piece of candy he said the child had not paid for. When he learned of the incident, Ken Rex became enraged. The clerk apologized.

Ken Rex apparently brooded over the matter for days. Finally, he drove his pickup truck into the alley behind Bowencamp's store. Bowencamp was on his back porch, cutting the tops off cardboard milk crates to put the milk in refrigerators. His big cooler had broken down in the midst of a hot spell. Ken Rex took out his shotgun and fired at Bowencamp, wounding him.

"Just shot him," said Sheriff's Deputy Ross Johnson. "He said the old man threatened him with a knife — a seventy-two-year-old man with a cardboard cutter."

Once again Ken Rex was arrested and charged with assault. A judge ruled the trial had to be moved to another county because it would be impossible to find an impartial jury in Nodaway County.

Because Ken Rex's lawyer was able to win one delay after another, the case didn't come to trial for nearly a year. Ken Rex's defense was that the old man had attacked him with a knife (the cardboard cutter). But the jury thought differently. Ken Rex was convicted of assault with intent to kill and given a two-year sentence. It was his first conviction.

The people of Skidmore had hoped that Ken Rex would receive a much longer sentence. But at least he would be off the streets for a while.

However, Ken Rex's lawyer filed an appeal, meaning a higher court would review the conviction and sentence. Ken Rex, who had yet to spend a day in jail, was freed on $60,000 bond until the appeal could be heard.

"He was right back in town, free as can be," said one Skidmore farmer. "That's what got everybody so mad, and the way the police would keep arresting him and the courts kept letting him go."

The anger was mixed with fear. The witnesses who had testified against Ken Rex got especially jittery.

Four nights after his release, Ken Rex walked into the D&G Tavern followed by his twenty-four-year-old wife, Trina, who carried an M-1 rifle with a bayonet. During the evening, Ken Rex made some threatening remarks about "old man Bowencamp" and took the rifle from his wife. Everyone in the tavern knew that by so doing, Ken Rex had violated the terms of his bond. For that he could be jailed.

Two weeks later, a judge was to hear arguments as to whether Ken Rex's bond should be cancelled because he was seen with a rifle. On the morning of the hearing, about sixty of Skidmore's townspeople gathered downtown. They planned on going to the courthouse as a group because they felt a big crowd might impress the judge.

Then word came that the hearing had been

postponed. The townspeople were angry and frustrated. They gathered at the American Legion Hall and invited the sheriff. They wanted to discuss what to do next about protecting themselves from Ken Rex.

The sheriff sought to calm the crowd. He assured the townspeople that he and his deputies would keep an eye on things.

Deputy Owens would later say that nothing went on at the meeting to indicate that anyone was planning to harm Ken Rex. "It was basically more or less a neighborhood watch program," Owens said.

The sheriff had left, and the meeting had about run its course when someone broke in with an ominous message: "McElroy's in town."

It was true. Ken Rex had driven his pickup into Skidmore and parked in front of the D&G Tavern. His wife was with him. They went into the bar. He ordered beer, and his wife had soda.

Many of the men who had attended the meeting at the American Legion Hall decided to go over to the D&G and confront Ken Rex. They stood on the street outside, waiting. "They were staring," Mrs. McElroy would later tell police, "and they were silent."

When Ken Rex and his wife came out of the tavern to get into the pickup, the men of Skidmore encircled the truck. Mrs. McElroy climbed in on the passenger side. Then Ken Rex started to get in behind the wheel.

As Ken Rex reached for the ignition key, his

wife screamed. Someone across the street had raised a rifle. "They've got a gun!" Trina shrieked.

Shots rang out. McElroy fell dead, struck by two bullets through the head.

At the sound of the shots, everyone scattered. Although the street had been crowded before the shooting, minutes after it was completely empty. Trina, fearing for her own life, had fled into the bank.

The shooting shook Skidmore. The townspeople didn't want to talk about what people called "the incident," not even among themselves.

Someone washed away the blood and the chalked outline of McElroy's body the police had drawn on the blacktop street in front of the D&G.

Of the crowd that had surrounded McElroy's pickup, not one person came forward to say who had fired the shots. "The whole bunch of them was there and they all saw it," said Trina McElroy. "They were all in on it."

A coroner's jury investigated the killing. Mrs. McElroy told the jury she saw who shot her husband and gave the man's name. Nevertheless, no arrest warrant was issued. The jury concluded that Ken Rex was killed by a "person or persons unknown."

Said Lois Bowencamp, wife of the man McElroy had shot, "Justice has been served."

Not everyone agreed. "A man was killed in the presence of sixty people," said Richard E. McFadden, who had been Ken Rex's attorney. "If people are allowed to violate the law this way, it's a tremendously bad example."

McFadden asked the FBI to investigate charges that local officials were covering up a conspiracy to kill McElroy. But nothing ever came of the request.

The story of the shooting was covered by newspapers and television stations in every part of the country. It was spotlighted on the CBS television program *60 Minutes*, covered in the book, *Judgment Day*, by Bob Lancaster and B.C. Hall, and was the subject of the TV movie *In Broad Daylight*, based on the book by Harry N. MacLean.

"Anyone who has spent time in the community will come away with the sense that most of the townspeople know, all right, who the killer is," said Lancaster and Hall. "And one gets the impression that those who don't know have deliberately avoided finding out: The knowledge would be a burden to have to live with."

When reporters visited Skidmore to interview residents, they found very few who expressed any regret or sorrow over what they called "the incident." "Whoever did it did everyone a favor," was a common attitude.

"All we want to do," said Lois Bowencamp, "is go back to doing what we do best, which is minding our own business."

Whatever Happened to Etan Patz?

Not long before eight o'clock on the gray morning of May 25, 1979, a six-year-old, blue-eyed, blond-haired boy named Etan Patz, carrying a book bag with elephants imprinted on it, kissed his mother good-bye and started walking toward his school-bus stop.

In the Soho section of New York City where Etan lived, the noisy, narrow streets are clogged with trucks and cars at that time of day. But the sidewalks have only a few pedestrians.

Etan had to walk less than two blocks to the bus stop. He knew the route by heart, for he and his mother had covered it many times. But Etan had never walked it alone. For weeks, he had begged to be allowed to go himself. On that misty morning late in May 1979, Mrs. Patz gave in.

She stood in the doorway at 113 Prince Street as Etan made his way down the block. When he reached the intersection where Prince met Wooster Street, she turned and went back inside to climb the three flights of stairs to the family's apartment.

Mr. Patz was still sleeping. Etan's younger brother, Ari, two years old, had had an overnight guest and they were up and playing. The family's oldest child, Shira, eight years old, was getting ready for school.

Mrs. Patz felt Etan would be fine. At the time, Soho was a close-knit neighborhood of loft apartments, small factories, art galleries, and shops. The Patzes' children knew many people in the neighborhood. Mothers and other children would be waiting at the bus stop.

A woman neighbor saw Etan carrying his school bag and wearing his black Future Flight Captain cap at the corner of Prince and Wooster. A mailman saw him at the same intersection, waiting to cross.

Etan was one block from his destination, the school-bus stop on West Broadway. He never made it.

At eight o'clock that morning, the yellow school bus arrived to pick up the children clustered at the stop and deliver them to Independence Plaza School on Greenwich Street and the Hudson River. Etan was not among them. His teacher noted his absence but did not report it. School regulations did not require her to do so.

At the end of the school day, the bus picked up the children and dropped them at the West Broadway stop. A neighbor always met Etan at the stop, along with her own daughter. She then dropped Etan at his door.

When Etan did not arrive home at the usual

time that afternoon, Mrs. Patz became concerned. She called the neighbor who always picked him up and learned he had not been on the bus. The neighbor's daughter said he had not been in class, either. Mrs. Patz called other parents, whose children also said that Etan had not been in class. She called the school and was told he had never arrived.

Now Mrs. Patz was terrified. She called the police and then her husband, a photographer, at work.

"I was just coming home from a business trip at around five o'clock in the afternoon," a neighbor recalled, "when I ran into Stan [Mr. Patz]. He was walking up and down Prince Street, looking around, and he was tense. 'Etan's not back from school yet,' he said."

A police car arrived at the Patz apartment early in the evening. The two officers asked to see a picture of Etan. They asked routine questions about friends, relatives, and people who Etan might have spoken to on his way to the bus stop. Mrs. Patz told the officers that her son was very friendly and trusting.

Detective Bill Butler, one of the two officers, believed the case was not routine, not a case where the child was with a close friend, had wandered off somewhere, or played hooky. Butler phoned his superiors and asked for assistance.

That night nearly one hundred policemen and detectives from Manhattan were assigned to search Soho buildings and interview residents. Police cars, their lights flashing, lined the streets in front of the Patz apartment, which became a command post. Cops with flashlights searched rooftops and poked through basements. It was the beginning of what was to become one of the longest and widest manhunts in city history.

"Every loft in the area was gone through not once, but three times," a resident recalled, "right down to the bottom of our bureau drawers."

The other Patz children were bewildered. Ari, who shared a bunk bed with Etan, seemed frightened by all of the activity. Mrs. Patz later learned that little Ari thought Etan had done something terribly wrong by getting lost, and the police were trying to find him to put him in jail.

The next day, police helicopters inspected rooftops from Fourteenth Street to the lower tip of Manhattan Island. Police launches checked the waterways and shorelines.

The police also tried bloodhounds. The dogs were given the scent of Etan's pajamas. Unfortunately, rain had fallen during the night, which made finding Etan's trail more difficult. Three times the bloodhounds seemed to have picked up Etan's path but each time, the path led nowhere.

The *New York Daily News* featured a story and picture of Etan. Afterward, special telephone lines that had been installed in the Patz apartment by police were jammed with calls that continued for days. People thought they had seen Etan on streets, in stores, parks, and on subways and buses.

New Yorkers weren't the only ones who called. Since the story was also carried in the *Daily News*'s out-of-town edition, calls also came from places like New Milford, Connecticut, Skokie, Illinois, and Petaluma, California.

Hundreds of police and detectives followed up on all of the reported sightings. In the case of calls from outside New York, the New York police contacted local police. But none of the leads led anywhere.

The day after Etan vanished, the first of hundreds of psychics called on one of the special telephone lines. Each claimed to have information about Etan based on his or her supernatural powers.

Some of the psychics said a man took Etan; some said a woman took him. Some said he was alive; some said he was dead. A Long Island psychic said he had a vision of Etan standing on the corner of Broadway and Eighteenth Street. Police searched the area, but there was no sign of him.

Detectives were hopeful when another psychic said she had seen Etan standing by a window, rubbing his hands together. She went on to portray the scene in careful detail. She described a bridge outside the apartment, a street with an iron railing on one side, and a certain type of car parked at a certain spot. Her vision even included the street name. Police rushed to the site. The scene was exactly as the psychic had described it. Every apartment was searched. Every tenant was shown Etan's picture. But no one had seen him.

A few psychics felt Etan's disappearance had been brought about by someone who had a grudge against Mr. and Mrs. Patz. When the Patzes were asked about this, they were unable to name anyone who bore ill toward them. They offered to be put under hypnosis in an effort to identify such a person. But even in a hypnotic trance, they could not name any known enemy.

Those who claimed to have visions of Etan or to have spoken to God about him frequently called during the early morning hours. Nevertheless, the Patzes never discouraged the calls. In fact, they kept their telephone number listed because they believed there might be a chance that such people might turn out to know something.

Two days after Etan's disappearance, a woman reported seeing a boy about Etan's age talking to a "suspicious looking" man on a street corner only three blocks from where Etan had last been seen. Under hypnosis, the woman put together a detailed picture of a tall, white male, about forty years old, with dyed blond hair, and freckles on his face.

Using the description, a police department artist prepared a sketch of the man. When the sketch was released to newspapers and television stations, scores of people came forward to say they knew the man or had seen him. Each person, however, had a different candidate.

The detectives interviewed half a dozen men who resembled the artist's drawing. "I looked at a guy, and I looked back at the sketch, and I looked back at the guy, and I just couldn't believe it," Detective Butler said. "The next day, there was the sketch all over again. Everybody's starting to look like the sketch."

Friends and Soho neighbors of the Patzes formed the Etan Patz Action Committee to spearhead the search. The Committee focused on getting posters printed and distributed.

Designed by a neighbor and printed as a gift by Soho printers, the poster featured one of Mr. Patz's photographs of a smiling Etan, who was described as being forty inches tall and weighing fifty pounds. The posters were printed in five languages — English, Spanish, Chinese, Yiddish, and Italian.

Volunteers handled the distribution of the posters, traveling by foot, subway, or bus, throughout the New York Metropolitan area. Before long, Etan's image was looking down from thousands of walls and windows.

Volunteers pleaded with television stations to have the poster shown on local newscasts. They sought to have the poster reprinted in area newspapers.

Newspapers were helpful for the most part. But one story deeply pained the Patzes. A paper printed a rumor that Etan had been seen in the Boston area, where his parents had originally come from. Readers were given the impression that Etan was safe and sound with his paternal grandparents.

As a result, people began taking down posters. But the story was totally false. Mr. Patz got very angry and upset about it.

Some two weeks after Etan disappeared, the emergency response ended. The hundreds of detectives and police officers were reassigned to other crimes. The special phone lines were removed from the Patz apartment.

But Detective Butler and three other detectives from the Missing Persons Bureau stayed on as a special task force.

They continued to trace down every lead. They questioned hundreds of people who might have seen something. But all the leads led nowhere.

October 9, 1979, was Etan's seventh birthday. Almost five months had passed since he had vanished. There was no celebrating at the Patz apartment. Etan's parents remained near the telephone in hopes of hearing news about their son.

Both Mr. and Mrs. Patz were convinced that Etan was still alive. "We still think some misguided person who wanted to have a beautiful little boy took Etan," Mrs. Patz told *The New York Times*. "We keep praying that person will have pity on us and return our son."

The Patzes published Etan's pictures in *Search*, a catalog of missing children that is distributed nationally to police, hospitals, and social service agencies. They registered with Child Find, Inc., an organization that circulates a toll-free number across the country that any abducted child can call for help.

Many people urged the Patzes to make an effort to raise money for a reward fund for Etan's return.

At first, they declined to do so. They were worried that offering a reward might encourage someone to take another child and hold him or her hostage.

By 1981, however, the Patzes had overcome their fears about a reward fund. "We still don't like the idea," said Mrs. Patz, "but it's about the only thing we have left to do."

The following year, 1982, a $25,000 reward was offered by Etan's parents. Mr. Patz explained the reward would be given for "credible information" leading to Etan's return or proof that he was dead. The reward was provided by a donor who wished to remain anonymous, Mr. Patz said.

The same year, a retired New York City cab driver came forth to report that he believed he had picked up Etan and a man near the boy's home on the day he disappeared at about the time he was on his way to the school bus. Why hadn't the cab driver reported this important evidence at the time? The police said he had withheld the information because of personal problems and the fear that the criminal might harm him.

This new lead helped to renew efforts to find Etan. But it came to nothing.

The New York City Police Department, which continued to keep two detectives assigned to the case, operated on the basis that Etan was still alive. "Somewhere out there is someone who knows something," said one detective. But everyone involved with the case fully realized the chances of ever finding Etan diminished with each passing day.

In leading the search for Etan, the Patzes helped to accomplish one great good. At the time of the boy's disappearance, the public had little interest in the subject of missing children. There were no private organizations or government agencies to help bring children back. The Patzes helped change that.

They joined with parents of other lost children and political officials sympathetic to their cause to raise a "chorus of voices" on behalf of missing children. There's plenty of evidence as to what they were able to achieve. For instance, pictures of missing children now appear on milk cartons, shopping bags, and highway toll tickets.

"Our shock in the beginning," said Mr. Patz, "was how easy it was to abduct a child and get away with it. The National Crime Information Center's computer, Mr. Patz pointed out, kept statistics on stolen cars, but not on missing children.

In 1982, President Ronald Reagan signed the Missing Children Act. It required the FBI to accept the records of missing children on their computer.

In 1984, with a $4 million grant from the Department of Justice, the National Center for Missing and Exploited Children opened in Washington, D.C. It instructs people to call its toll-free number — (800) 843–5678 — to report a case of a missing child or to report a sighting of a missing child.

The National Center for Missing and Exploited Children says that many crimes against children can be prevented. It issues basic safety rules children should be taught to protect themselves from abduction and exploitation. They include the following:

• If you are in a public place, and you get separated from your parents, don't wander around looking for them. Go to the checkout counter, the security office, or the lost and found and quickly tell the person in charge that you have lost your mom and dad and need help in finding them.

• You should not get into a car or go anywhere with any person unless your parents have told you it is okay.

• If someone follows you on foot or in a car, stay away from him or her. You don't need to go near the car to talk to people inside.

• Grownups and other older people who need help should not be asking children for help; they should be asking older people.

• No one should be asking you for directions, or asking you to help look for a "lost puppy," or telling you that your mother or father is in trouble and that he or she will take you to them.

• If someone tries to take you somewhere, quickly get away from her or him and yell or scream "This man (or woman) is trying to take me away," or "This person is not my father or mother."

• You should try to use the "buddy system" and never go places alone.

• Always ask your parents' permission to leave the yard or play area or to go into someone's home.

• No one should ask you to keep a special secret. If he or she does, tell your parents or teacher.

• No one should touch you on parts of the body covered by the bathing suit, nor should you touch anyone else in those areas. Your body is special and private.

• You can be assertive, and you have the right to say NO to someone who tries to take you somewhere, touches you, or makes you feel uncomfortable in any way.

In its efforts to prevent crimes against children, the National Center for Missing and Exploited Children also distributes photos and descriptions of missing children throughout the nation, publishes books and brochures to help educate the public about missing and exploited children, and helps train law enforcement officials in how to deal with missing-children cases.

May 25, 1989, the tenth anniversary of the misty spring morning when Etan went off to school, never to be seen again, passed without anything new to report. At the Missing Persons Bureau of the New York City Police Department, the Etan Patz case was still open. Leads still came in from people who believed they had seen Etan, and each was checked out.

"We've had thousands, literally thousands, of leads," said Lieutenant Robert Douglas, commander of the Missing Persons Squad. "But none of them have led to anything. We have four file cabinets full — *full* — just on this particular case."

But the efforts of law enforcement officials began to be hindered by the fact that Etan, described as forty inches tall and fifty pounds in the original "missing" posters, was now a teenager. There had been a drastic change in his appearance.

Mr. Patz recognized the problem. "We're still sending out pictures taken in March of 1979," he said. "It just doesn't work."

Working with a computer, a neighbor produced an image of what Etan might look like as a thirteen-year-old. The sketch was based on the appearances of other family members. However, the Patzes felt uneasy about distributing the picture. They feared it might not resemble their son and thus might actually hamper the search for him.

Mr. and Mrs. Patz still live in the same apartment on Prince Street, with their two other children, Shira and Ari.

People continue to call them occasionally to report a "sighting," Mr. Patz said. He passes on such information to the police. The detective in charge of the case calls the Patzes about once a week to brief them on new leads.

The Patzes' pain has hardly lessened through the years. "Of all the types of crime," said Mr. Patz, "this is perhaps the cruelest because there is

the tunnel ceiling. The last three coaches, blackened and with broken windows, lay on their sides in front of the platform.

All six coaches were packed with passengers. Some had been sitting, but most had been straphangers. They were people arriving in the banking and insurance center of London for their day's work.

The first passengers to be rescued were those who could be passed through the windows and blackened buckled doors of the three rear cars. Most had broken bones or suffered from cuts and bruises. And most, of course, were in a state of shock.

An emergency operating room was set up on the station platform. But some people died before doctors could reach them.

"It was like being in a mineshaft after an explosion," said one rescuer. "They came out looking as though they had been pulled through a sack of soot."

Only one newspaper reporter, a man from the *Daily Telegraph,* was allowed on the station platform. He described the scene as "like something out of a wartime film."

He said: "The platform was choked with helmeted firemen, police, ambulance workers, doctors, nurses, and welfare workers. The up escalator was working, bringing up black-faced and tired rescuers. Everybody was sweaty, ghastly, haggard, and filthy. And amidst the sounds of rescue I could

27

hear the sound of people laughing hysterically. The heat was intense; it must have been 120 degrees."

In the streets outside the station entrance, a fleet of ambulances waited for the dead and injured. Crowds of curious bystanders watched in silence.

Passengers told of being hurled to the floor when the train struck. Many were wedged in by buckled metal.

One victim, after receiving stitches for a large gash in his head, told what the crash was like from the passenger's point of view: "There was a small screech and then a large one. I fell flat on my face and cut myself. I could hear a woman screaming. It was pitch-black, and the air was filled with soot.

"Then people were picking themselves up and asking where they were and saying, 'Don't panic.' I tried to make for the back of the train and emergency lights came on. It took me a quarter of an hour to get out through the window. . . ."

Relatives of people who were thought to be in the train jammed police telephone lines seeking information about their loved ones. The police also received a great number of calls from people who wanted to volunteer their services. "People have been unbelievably good and helpful," said a police spokesperson. "We have had calls from people who want to do everything from nursing to mechanical work, to simply making cups of tea."

By midmorning, a work crew had set up lifting equipment and had begun to wrench the rear coaches back from those in front that had buckled into a tangle of metal at the end of the tunnel. It was slow going, an inch at a time. Once they had space, workers using acetylene torches began the slow and painful job of cutting through the mass of wreckage to reach the passengers. "I saw about six dead in the first car," said one doctor. "It was just a horrible mess of limbs and mangled iron."

There were only two survivors in the first car. One was a nineteen-year-old policewoman who was pinned to her seat by twisted wreckage. Only her head and shoulders were visible. She remained cheerful, talking with rescuers through a small microphone as they worked to reach her. Only after doctors amputated her left foot could the woman be freed.

When the rescue team reached the rear of the first car, workers were unable to start cutting because they feared the massive steel wheels of the second coach, which were poised over it, would come crashing down on top of them. Work was halted until a crane could be brought in to hoist the wheels off the car roof.

The death toll mounted steadily. It was twenty-three by the end of the first day. It was forty-two by the time the rescuers had finished — at the end of the fifth day. Some eighty people were injured. It was the worst disaster in the one hundred-year-old history of the London subway system.

Almost from the moment of the crash, people began to speculate on what had caused it. One theory suggested the driver might have had a heart attack or stroke, and then collapsed.

But officials pointed out that even if the driver had lost consciousness for some reason and released his grip on the controls, the train would have stopped. That's because it was equipped with what is known as a "dead-man's brake." This device automatically stops the train when pressure on the throttle is released. It works something like a doorbell, that is, when you take your finger off the button, the bell stops ringing.

When newspaper reporters asked J. Graeme Bruce, the London subway's chief operating officer, why the train had crashed, he said it appeared that there had been "a lack of application of the brakes." Everyone knew that. Bruce's answer simply raised more questions. Why hadn't the brakes been applied? Had there been a mechanical failure? Or had there been a failing on the part of the driver?

Once the death toll had been established and the clearing of the wreckage completed, reporters became more and more curious about the driver of the train, who was also among the casualties. His name was Leslie Newson. He was fifty-five years old, married, a quiet man, and one who seemed to love his job.

In March and April that year, when public inquiries into the tragedy were held, a picture emerged of Newson as a careful, even cautious, driver. A guard on the train that crashed testified that he always felt safe when traveling with Newson. The guard explained that Newson, when coming into a station, would always "let it [the train] coast before he started to brake."

Raymond Deedman, a driving instructor, said that Newson had driven trains into the Moorgate Station on 121 previous occasions. "He drove slower than the average driver," Deedman stated.

Newson's dedication to his job was underscored by a notebook found in his possession. It was filled with instructions on how to deal with any defects that might occur in mechanical equipment. Other papers Newson carried gave advice on how he should personally conduct himself on the railway. "In my view," said Charles Cope, an assistant manager of the subway line, "these are indications of an employee who intended to carry out his job in a conscientious manner."

Another official testified as to how Newson always wore a full uniform. "He loved the job very much and told me it was the best job he had ever worked on," said the official.

The inquiry also established that Newson was fit and normal on the morning of the crash. His wife testified that he had given her the usual "peck on the cheek" before leaving for work. None of his coworkers could recall anything unusual in his behavior.

But there was also disturbing testimony concerning Newson. Twenty-one-year-old Anthony Board, a postal worker, was waiting on the platform as the train with Newson at the controls roared into the station. It was clear to Board that the train was going too fast. When he glanced at Newson, he saw that he was "paralyzed and frozen in his driving position."

Perhaps the last person to see Newson alive, Board said: "I saw him sitting upright with both of his arms forward; his right hand was on the dead man's handle. His eyes seemed to be staring straight ahead and seemed to be larger than life."

Keith Simpson, a professor of forensic medicine at London University, examined Newson's body. He said that the driver had been alive at the time of the crash.

Injuries to Newson's left hand seemed to indicate he had been gripping some object. The heel of his right hand appeared to have been resting in a position that suggested he was grasping a large circular knob. In other words, Newson seemed to have been holding the controls normally.

"I found no disease of any kind whatever, nor any suggestion of drink or drugs," said Simpson. "There was nothing to suggest an epileptic fit, a heart attack, or brain damage."

Then came a bombshell. Dr. Ann Robinson, a staff member of the London Hospital Medical College and one of Britain's leading experts on the effects of poisons on the human body, testified that Newson had been drinking before the crash. Her test showed, she testified, that Newson's blood contained alcohol, an amount indicating he might have consumed several ounces of whiskey.

Newson may not have been drunk, according to Dr. Robinson, but the alcohol could have slowed his responses. "He could be put almost in a state of trance," another doctor testified.

Dr. Robinson's testimony came only minutes after Mrs. Newson, the driver's widow, had collapsed on the witness stand after giving evidence about her husband and his drinking habits.

"Do you know," she was asked, "if he ever took a tot of spirits to keep the cold out at 4 A.M. on a winter's morning?"

"He never did," she answered. "My husband did not like spirits. He did not like whiskey or anything like that. All he liked was brown ale."

Earlier, Mrs. Newson had said her husband enjoyed half a pint of brown ale after an evening meal. She could not recall whether he had a drink of brown ale the night before the accident.

"There were certainly spirits in the house," she said. "Bacardi and things like that for festive occasions like Christmas, but he never touched them. He didn't like spirits."

Four of Newson's coworkers testified that on the morning of the accident there was no evidence he had been drinking. He appeared quite normal.

Herbert Laing, a motorman, said, "Before we went on duty, Mr. Newson gave me some milk from his bottle for my tea. It tasted quite normal. There was no taste of whiskey, rum, or other liquor, but I only had a little drop."

Then another expert witness took the stand to explain that alcohol levels in the blood can rise sharply through biochemical changes that take place if the blood is not stored in a refrigerator. Other experts took the witness stand to agree with this statement, concluding there was no certain way to establish how much alcohol, if any, had been in Newson's bloodstream at the time of his death, and how much formed after he died.

A footnote to the tragedy concerned nineteen-year-old Robert Harris, a guard on the train. Harris's job was to keep aware of the train's speed as it entered or left the station. If the train approached a station at too high a speed, Harris, seated at a control panel, was to apply an emergency brake.

On the morning of the crash, as the train was entering Moorgate Station, Harris, wanting something to read, left his post to search through the cars for a discarded newspaper. "I didn't even know we were approaching Moorgate," Harris testified.

The investigations also focused upon the train's braking system. To stop the train, Newson had only to move a handle on his left. This applied the electro-pneumatic brakes.

If this had failed, he simply would have had to pull the handle a little farther. Then an automatic air brake would have taken hold. But Newson had made no attempt to apply the brakes.

The jury hearing the evidence deliberated for just over an hour. Their verdict: accidental death.

In other words, the jurors could find no reason why Leslie Newson, always a careful, conscientious trainsman, had driven blindly toward the tunnel's end, a wall "as solid as a granite cliff," as one witness described it.

Were Newson's senses dulled by drugs or alcohol? Did he suffer some physical breakdown that went undetected by medical experts? Did he crack up mentally? Or was there simply some mechanical mishap that caused the brakes of the speeding train to fail? No one can say.

Who Shot Robert Kennedy?

For America, 1968 was a violent year. On April 4, the Reverend Martin Luther King, Jr., who, as the founder and president of the Southern Christian Leadership Conference, had been in the forefront of the civil rights movement for more than a decade, was shot to death in Memphis, Tennessee. James Earl Ray, an escaped convict, pleaded guilty to the slaying.

The Vietnam War raged throughout 1968. President Lyndon Johnson had committed hundreds of thousands of American troops to the fighting. Nightly television newscasts were showing American soldiers fighting and dying in the jungles of Southeast Asia. Those opposed to the war and America's involvement held demonstrations, marches, and silent vigils without letup.

President Johnson and his policies were even challenged by members of his own party, particularly by Minnesota Senator Eugene McCarthy. Although he was little known at the time, McCarthy ran against Johnson in the New Hampshire presidential primary in 1968. While he didn't win, McCarthy's unexpected strong race showed that Johnson could be beaten.

Four days after the New Hampshire primary, New York Senator Robert F. Kennedy, brother to President John F. Kennedy who had been assassinated in 1963, announced that he, too, would be a presidential candidate. Kennedy declared his wish "to seek new policies, to close the gaps between black and white, rich and poor, young and old in this country and around the world." Kennedy received strong backing from many of his brother's former supporters.

Through the spring, McCarthy and Kennedy battled in the primaries with no clear winner. The California primary, held early in June, was seen as crucial to both candidates. "If we lose here," a Kennedy campaign worker said, "we can all go home."

Kennedy and his staff worked hard in California. On the last day of the campaign, Kennedy put in fourteen hours. That night he slipped away to Malibu, where six of his ten children were staying in a beachfront home. He spent the morning bodysurfing with them. Late in the day, he returned to his campaign headquarters at the Hotel Ambassador in Los Angeles, arriving at about the time election results started coming in.

When it became clear that he was going to win the election, Kennedy made his way from his fifth-floor suite to the Embassy ballroom to deliver his victory speech to campaign workers and supporters. With him as he went were his wife, Ethel, a group of close friends, plus members of his staff.

It was shortly after midnight when Kennedy began to speak. After thanking a long list of people, with his comments bringing laughs and cheers, Kennedy ended by saying, "I think we can end the divisions in the United States . . . we can work together. We are a great country, a selfless . . . and a compassionate country . . . So my thanks to you, and on to Chicago [where the Democratic National Convention was to be held in August], and let's win."

Next on Kennedy's schedule was a press conference that had been arranged by his staff, to be held on the same floor as the ballroom. Rather than try to struggle through the dense ballroom crowd to get to the press conference, Kennedy agreed to take a shortcut through the hotel kitchen.

When he had finished his speech, Kennedy parted the gold curtains at the rear of the platform to enter a corridor leading to the kitchen area. He was surrounded by a crowd of staff members and friends.

Karl Uecker, the assistant *maître d'hôtel*, and Edward Minasian, another hotel employee, cleared the way for the senator and his party. As he passed through the kitchen, the help lined up to Kennedy's left, and he began shaking hands with them, moving with kind of a sideways shuffle.

Just ahead, waiting for Kennedy in a serving pantry through which the senator had to pass, was a twenty-four-year-old immigrant from Jordan, Sirhan Bishara Sirhan. A nervous and hostile young man, Sirhan was extremely anti-Semitic, and was known to fly into blind rages against Israel and the Jews. Sirhan apparently identified Kennedy with American policy in the Middle East and the nation's support of Israel.

Twice Sirhan had been turned away from the ballroom where Kennedy had spoken because he had no credentials. He had then slipped into the kitchen, where he had gone unnoticed among the cooks, waiters, busboys, and dishwashers, plus campaign workers who were hoping to catch a glimpse of Kennedy.

In one hand, Sirhan clutched a Kennedy campaign poster. Behind the poster he concealed a fully loaded Cadet model .22 caliber Iver-Johnson revolver.

When Kennedy came into the pantry, Sirhan took the gun out from behind the poster, pointed it at Kennedy's head, and started firing. The gun went *pop!* Then a pause, then *pop!* again, then a third time.

Kennedy slumped backward. Other people fell to the floor. Women screamed.

Uecker turned, saw what had happened, and leapt for Sirhan. He managed to get one arm around his neck while he grappled for the gun with the other hand. He and Minasian slammed Sirhan against a stainless-steel serving table. Uecker seized the gun hand and began pounding it on the table top.

But he could not make Sirhan stop shooting. The revolver kept going *pop! pop! pop!* until its eight chambers were empty.

Uecker and Minasian shoved Sirhan into another table. Then Roosevelt Grier, 6 feet 5, 285 pounds, a former pro football lineman, and close friend of the Kennedys, surged into the struggle, toppling the three men to the floor.

The revolver finally tumbled free. Rafer Johnson, another Kennedy friend and an Olympic gold medalist, pounced on it.

Kennedy, meanwhile, lay flat on his back, his arms out, his legs slightly bent. Two bullets had entered his body beneath his arm. One of them lodged near the base of his neck. A third shattered a small bone behind his right ear and then angled toward his brain.

Juan Romero, a seventeen-year-old busboy, knelt down beside Kennedy. He cradled his head in one hand and gave him a crucifix.

A radio reporter wandered through the crowd. He seemed bewildered. "Senator Kennedy has been shot," he said into his tape recorder. "Senator Kennedy has been shot. Is that possible? Is that possible? It is possible, ladies and gentlemen, it is possible, he has."

Kennedy was not the only person to have been struck down. The pantry was filled with wounded. William Weisel, a thirty-year-old production assistant for ABC-TV, slumped in a corner, clutching at where a bullet had entered his belly. Elizabeth

Evans, forty-three, had fallen to the floor after a bullet had grazed her scalp, spilling blood down her face. Paul Schrade, forty-three, an official with the United Auto Workers union, also had a head wound. Seventeen-year-old Irwin Stroll had been shot in the calf. Still another stray bullet had caught Ira Goldstein, nineteen, in the thigh. "Will you help me?" he kept asking people. "Will you help me? I've been shot."

Police in helmets wedged their way through the throng to seize Sirhan from the men who were holding him. Picking him up by the arms, they ran him downstairs and out of the hotel and into a waiting squad car. The car sped away, its light flashing, its siren screaming.

By now Ethel Kennedy had fought her way through the crush and dropped to her knees at her husband's side. The crowd pressed in from every side. "Give him air!" Mrs. Kennedy pleaded. "Give him air!"

An ambulance arrived from Central Receiving Hospital. The attendants gently lifted Kennedy onto a stretcher, rolled the stretcher to a freight elevator, then out to a waiting ambulance. Blood poured from his head wound, and his heartbeat was faint.

At the hospital's emergency room, a medical team worked over him and there were signs of recovery. Doctors decided to send him to the better-equipped Hospital of the Good Samaritan, four blocks away. But neither the doctors nor the equipment could save him. Robert Kennedy died early the next morning.

Sirhan freely confessed to the murder and was convicted and sentenced to death. He escaped this fate, however, when the Supreme Court abolished capital punishment in 1972.

At the present, Sirhan remains in California's San Quentin Prison, where he is serving a life sentence. He has hopes that one day he may be cleared of the murder conviction and given his freedom.

Americans were quick to accept Sirhan as the one and only gunman. In the minds of many, he was another "lone nut" — like Lee Harvey Oswald, who was charged with the assassination of President John F. Kennedy, in 1963, and James Earl Ray, who was found guilty in the murder of Martin Luther King, Jr.

Nevertheless, many doubts have been raised in connection with Robert Kennedy's murder and they have persisted to this day. More than a few journalists, criminologists, public officials, and eyewitnesses to the shooting have questioned and continue to question much of the evidence that led to Sirhan being named the only gunman.

Take, for instance, the testimony of several of the fifty or so persons who were crowded into the serving pantry at the time of the shooting. None of the witnesses who testified at Sirhan's trial placed Kennedy closer than two feet to Sirhan when he began to fire. And some witnesses declared the two men were separated by eight to ten feet.

Other evidence, however, disputes these eye-witness accounts. DeWayne Wolfer, a criminologist with the Los Angeles Police Department, and who once headed the department's crime laboratory, conducted chemical tests on the jacket the Senator was wearing the night of the shooting. The jacket bore the entry marks of three bullets. The tests showed the bullets were fired from a gun only a few inches away. Such evidence has led many people to accept a "two gun" theory in the Kennedy assassination.

There is also laboratory evidence to support this claim. Seven of the eight .22 caliber bullets fired from Sirhan's gun were recovered by police. In 1970, the bullets were studied and photographed by William H. Harper, a highly respected California criminologist.

According to Harper, one of the bullets removed from Kennedy's body did not appear to have been fired from the same pistol as the bullet removed from William Weisel, one of the wounded victims. Mr. Harper pointed out there was an important difference in the striations, the marks left on the bullets by the spiral grooving inside the gun barrel. These differences indicated to Harper that the bullets were fired by different weapons.

Other investigators have concentrated on how many bullets were fired. Official police reports state that eight bullets caused all the damage. Kennedy was shot three times. The five other victims were each shot once.

Seven of the eight bullets from Sirhan's gun were recovered, according to the Los Angeles Police Department. One that pierced Kennedy's body was lost in the ceiling space of the pantry.

But these findings have been disputed, most recently by Dan E. Moldea, a Washington, D.C., writer. Late in 1989, Moldea questioned investigators from the Los Angeles Police Department and Sheriff's Office who had been assigned to the case, calling them, "the most objective and experienced witnesses available."

Moldea asked the officers two questions: "What did you do?" and "What did you see?"

Sergeant James R. MacArthur, the senior detective from the Los Angeles Police Department at the scene, told Moldea that he had seen "quite a few" bullet holes. One, he remembered, hit high on the wall to the left of the swinging doors at the west end of the pantry, which would have been in Sirhan's line of fire.

Lieutenant Albin S. Hegge, who cataloged information from the murder scene, also remembered bullets being recovered. He said, "I know there were some, because they took out [door panels] . . . cut them out and saved them . . ."

Another officer recalled small evidence packages marked either "bullet evidence" or "firearms evidence." A police photographer remembered taking pictures of bullet holes.

Other investigators who contributed evidence included:

- William A. Bailey, an FBI special agent. Bailey signed a statement in 1976 that stated: "At one point . . . I (and several other agents) noted at least two (2) small-caliber bullet holes in the center post of the two doors leading from the preparation room [the pantry]. There was no question in any of our minds as to the fact that they were bullet holes."

- Alfred C. Grenier, an FBI special agent. Grenier conducted a survey of the crime scene after the shooting. His report identified four bullet holes in the door frames of the pantry. The report included photographs of the bullet holes taken by an FBI photographer.

- Walter Tew, Deputy, Los Angeles Sheriff's Office. Tew, who died in 1988, inspected the crime scene after the shooting and found four bullet holes in two door frames. He marked the evidence by circling each of the holes and scrawling his name, "W. Tew," badge number, "723," and "LASO" (for Los Angeles Sheriff's Office) inside each circle.

- Thomas Beringer, Deputy, Los Angeles Sheriff's Office. Beringer was one of the first law enforcement officers to arrive at the scene. He told Moldea: "I remember one person trying to take a bullet out of the [door frame] with a knife, a silver knife, for a souvenir."

The results of Moldea's investigation were published in the *Washington Post* in 1990. He concluded: ". . . there are strong reasons to believe that more than eight bullets were fired that night." In fact, added Moldea, ". . . current evidence suggests that 12 or more bullets may have been fired."

Eight bullets were the number that could be loaded into Sirhan's Iver-Johnson .22 caliber revolver. If Dan Moldea is right and more than eight bullets were fired, they had to have come from a second gun. If that's true, Sirhan did not act alone.

Through the years, those who support the second-gun theory have asked that the investigation of the assassination be reopened. Joseph Busch, the Los Angeles County District Attorney when such requests were made, resisted such efforts. He felt that examining the evidence a second time would not prove anything.

"The two-gun theory is a fictitious theory," Busch said.

"There is no question in our minds," Busch added, "that Sirhan Sirhan was the murderer of Robert Kennedy and that he acted alone."

Yet the doubts persist. The eyewitness accounts of the assassination seem to contradict one another. There is physical evidence that points to the possibility that more than one gun was fired.

Few doubt that Sirhan fired bullets that entered Robert Kennedy's body. But there is a strong reason to believe he did not act alone.

* * *

A final note. The Democratic presidential candidate in 1968 was not Eugene McCarthy, Robert Kennedy's principal challenger in the California primary, but Vice-President Hubert Humphrey.

In the general election that November, Humphrey was defeated by Republican Richard Nixon.

Movieland Mystery

During the mid-1920s, beautiful Thelma Todd went from being a sixth-grade schoolteacher in Lawrence, Massachusetts, to stardom as a movie actress. A fresh, vibrant, young woman, she was described by one critic as "the loveliest blonde ever seen on the screen." Her success, however, stemmed more from her talent for comedy than her good looks.

After she won a hometown beauty contest and the title "Miss Massachusetts," Thelma was offered a contract with Paramount Pictures. She attended the studio's school for motion picture acting in Astoria, New York, and then headed out to Hollywood.

There she starred in a series of "two reel" comedies, which were short features, nineteen minutes in length, that featured rough-and-tumble comedy — crashing dishes, car chases, collisions, and plenty of other kinds of loud, boisterous action. "Toddy," as her friends called her, also played comedy leads opposite Buster Keaton and Laurel and Hardy, giants of the screen in the 1920s and 1930s. She starred in two films with the fabled Marx Brothers, *Horse Feathers* and *Monkey Business,* both of which have remained popular to this day.

By 1935, Thelma Todd had completed about seventy films and reigned as one of the most successful actresses of the time. Two films in which she had starring roles, *All American Toothache* and *Bohemian Girl,* were soon to be released.

Highly paid, the actress had begun to invest her earnings. One of her ventures was what had become a popular restaurant, Thelma Todd's Roadside Rest, located on winding Roosevelt Highway (now known as the Pacific Coast Highway), which edged the Pacific Ocean between Santa Monica and Malibu.

Thelma's business partner was Roland West, a former boyfriend. She and West each had an apartment above the restaurant.

On Saturday evening, December 14, 1935, Thelma was the guest of honor at a party given in her honor by English comedian Stanley Lupino as a "thank-you" for having appeared in an English movie with him. The party was held at the Trocadero, a popular Hollywood nightclub. There were about twenty guests.

One of them was Pat DiCicco, Thelma's former husband. DiCicco was with another actress, Margaret Lindsay, that evening. He and Thelma got into a loud argument during the party.

Thelma left the nightclub at around two A.M., smiled and waved to her fans outside, and stepped into her limousine. She told her chauffeur, Ernest Peters, to drive her home.

The trip to Thelma's apartment was a frantic one. The actress, saying she feared she might be kidnapped or slain by gangsters, ordered Peters to drive at breakneck speed and not make any stops.

They arrived at the apartment not long before daybreak. Thelma dismissed the chauffeur, said good night, and got out of the car. The chauffeur drove off. He quite possibly was the last person to see Thelma Todd alive.

On Monday morning, Todd's maid, Mae Whitehead, came to work. When she was unable to find the actress in the apartment, she climbed the steep hill behind the restaurant to the garage where Thelma and Roland West kept their cars. There was the actress, slumped over the steering wheel of her chocolate-brown Lincoln convertible. She was wearing the same evening gown, the fur coat, and an array of jewelry she had been wearing when she left the Trocadero party more than thirty hours earlier.

The maid thought Thelma was sleeping and tried to rouse her. "Get up, honey," she said. "C'mon now, wake up, honey."

Suddenly she realized Thelma was not asleep. She ran from the garage, screaming, "She's dead! She's dead! Miss Todd's dead!"

In near panic, the maid hurried down the 270 concrete steps leading from the garage to the restaurant and awakened Roland West. When West saw Thelma's lifeless body, he telephoned the actress's doctor. The doctor, in turn, called the police.

The Los Angeles County Medical Examiner, A.F. Wagner, said the cause of death was carbon monoxide poisoning. This was his theory: After dismissing her chauffeur, Thelma found she didn't have her apartment keys with her. She was locked out. She then decided to climb the hill up to the garage, perhaps to rest in one of the cars. There was a chill in the air, and to keep warm she started the engine and turned on the heater. But she neglected to leave open the sliding garage door.

Thelma fell asleep with the engine running or was overcome by the fumes. In either case, the carbon monoxide killed her. The key was in the car's ignition, and the gas tank was empty.

Burial services for Thelma Todd were held at the Wee Kirk o' the Heather Chapel at the Forest Lawn Cemetery in Glendale, not far from Hollywood. The services were private, attended by Thelma's mother, Alice Todd, who lived nearby, Roland West, film stars ZaSu Pitts and Patsy Kelly, and a handful of other friends. Her body was cremated.

Meanwhile, a storm of controversy was raging over the circumstances of the actress's death. While it looked to be accidental, the medical examiner said that was not the case. "I believe the death to be suicide," he declared.

Thelma's friends insisted this couldn't be true,

that there was no reason why she would want to take her own life. She was happy and full of life, they said.

The trunk of Thelma's car was filled with Christmas presents she had told friends she would be delivering to them the following week. And she had posted signs on the front door of her restaurant announcing a gala New Year's party and the opening of a new third-floor dining room. Someone planning suicide wouldn't have been making such plans.

Alice Todd, the actress's mother, was angered by the medical examiner's statement. "Thelma Todd would never kill herself," she declared. "She was murdered. And I promise you this, I won't rest until the man who killed her is brought to justice."

Mrs. Todd's suggestion that Thelma might have been murdered sent shock waves through the Hollywood community. Police had no choice but to question those who might be considered suspects. Prominent on the list was the name of Thelma's business partner and ex-boyfriend, Roland West. Thelma's body had been found in the garage West shared with the actress.

According to police, Todd and West had quarreled on Saturday night when she was leaving the restaurant for the party.

"Was anything said about the time she was coming back?" police asked West.

"Well, I asked her jokingly to be back by two

o'clock," West said. "She said, smiling, 'five minutes after two.'

"I said, 'two o'clock.' She said, right back, 'five minutes after two,' and we repeated this several times. It was joking all the way."

According to rumors surrounding West, he was furious at Thelma for dumping him. Some neighbors said that they had heard a violent argument between West and Thelma on Sunday morning. Police, however, were never able to gather enough evidence to take West into custody and charge him with the crime.

There were other suspects besides West, however. There was Charles Smith, the treasurer of the restaurant corporation. Both Thelma and Roland West suspected that Smith was tampering with the restaurant records and pocketing money from the operation. Thelma planned to have another accountant examine the records after the first of the year.

Thelma's former husband, Pat DiCicco, was under suspicion, too. He had frequently exhibited his violent temper during his brief and stormy marriage to Thelma.

DiCicco had introduced Thelma to Charles "Lucky" Luciano, yet another suspect. A well-known gangster of the day, Luciano was believed to be pressuring Thelma to lease the restaurant for a gambling operation.

There was no doubt that there was a dark side to Thelma's life. She had received several letters during the year in which attempts had been made to extort money from her. One note demanded a $10,000 payment. If she refused, she would be killed. Another letter threatened to blow up her restaurant. Her chauffeur told police how, on the ride home early Sunday morning, Thelma had expressed great fear of gangsters.

The idea that Thelma might have been the victim of a violent crime was given some support by the condition of her body as described by the medical examiner. Her nose was broken; there was blood on her face, bruises on her neck, and she had two cracked ribs. Police shrugged off these injuries, however, saying they occurred when Thelma lurched forward and struck her head on the steering wheel.

There were so many questions to be answered, a grand jury investigation was ordered. Members of the jury would hear each witness and examine the evidence and then attempt to decide what caused the actress's death.

The jury convened on the fifth floor of Los Angeles's Hall of Justice, just six days before Christmas in 1935. The proceedings attracted huge throngs and scores of reporters from newspapers from every part of the country.

But instead of clearing up the mystery, the grand jury investigation deepened it. The strangest evidence came from several witnesses who claimed they had spoken to Thelma or actually seen her on Sunday afternoon or evening, hours after she was supposed to have died.

Mrs. Wallace Ford, a friend of Thelma's, told the grand jury she was "positive beyond question" that she had talked to Todd late Sunday afternoon. "I've known her for years and I couldn't be mistaken," Ford said.

"I had invited her to a cocktail party celebrating our anniversary," Ford declared. "Her maid telephoned me on Saturday to say she would come.

"Sunday afternoon, she telephoned me herself. She said, 'Darling, do you mind if I bring a guest?' I replied, 'Of course not, who is it?'

" 'You'll never guess, and you'll be surprised when you see,' she said.

"I told her I was dying of curiosity, but she wouldn't tell me anything more."

Another witness reported actually seeing Thelma. W.F. Persson, a cigar-store operator, testified that Thelma had entered his shop at about nine o'clock Sunday morning, hours after police believed the actress had died in the garage. "I was struck by her beauty," Persson said.

"She gave me a nickel and asked me to call a number for her," Persson continued. Persson even recalled the number he had dialed. "A minute or so later, a man came in and they left together," he said.

Persson also remembered how the woman he saw was dressed. She was wearing a full-length coat and a blue-sequined dinner gown. Her high-heeled blue shoes were "a little bit dirty," Persson recalled.

Jewel West, the former wife of Roland West,

Thelma's business partner, also testified she had seen the actress. She told the grand jury of having seen the actress in an automobile on Sunset Boulevard and Vine Street at about eleven o'clock Sunday night. She said Thelma was with "a man of dark complexion."

Such testimony bewildered the grand jury. Was it possible that Thelma Todd had been alive on Sunday night?

George Johnson, a Deputy District Attorney, lashed out at some of the witnesses, saying that they had testified for their own benefit, "for what they could get out of it." Johnson declared the investigation had become a "publicity bandwagon."

"It has resolved itself into a hodgepodge of honest evidence and obvious faking," Johnson declared. "We're having a hard time trying to sift one from the other."

In an effort to come to a clearer understanding of what had happened, members of the grand jury visited the site of the tragedy. One juror, after making the long climb up the steep hillside from Todd's apartment to the garage, shook his head in dismay. "That girl never made that climb," he said.

Another juror, after examining Roland West's apartment said, "It's impossible to believe he didn't hear her if she found herself locked out [of her own apartment] and rattled this door."

The jurors also inspected the garage. Todd's automobile stood exactly where it had been when her body was found. But neither the car nor the garage yielded any new clues.

Early in January 1936, when the grand jury handed down its verdict, it was obvious that the members of the panel were bewildered. Some believed that the actress had committed suicide, that she had known exactly what she was doing when she got into her car and switched on the ignition. Others thought Todd's death was an accident. A few clung to the theory that she had met with foul play.

Thelma Todd has not been forgotten. Her mysterious death was the subject of a book and a made-for-TV movie. And, in recent years, many of Thelma's comedy films have found a new audience on cable television. Her new fans appreciate Thelma for her beauty and comic skills. No doubt most are unaware of her tragic death and the confusion that surrounds it.

Nightmare

Intelligent. Gracious. Well-liked. Those were some of the words used to describe twenty-one-year-old Valerie Percy, one of the twin daughters of millionaire industrialist Charles H. Percy. She was striking in appearance — 5 feet 7, about 120 pounds, with blue eyes and blonde hair, and a sunny disposition. Valerie Percy's beauty could be noticed in any crowd, a friend once said of her.

When Valerie was killed by an intruder as she slept in the family mansion in Kenilworth, Illinois, not long before dawn on a September Sunday in 1956, the entire nation was shocked. *Time* magazine called it an "American nightmare."

"She was loved and admired by everyone in the community," said a neighbor of the Percys. "I'm so numb I can't believe what happened."

Violence was rare in Kenilworth, the mile-square community of about 3,000 some ten miles north of Chicago where the Percys lived. In fact, Valerie's slaying was the first murder in the seventy-five-year history of the town.

Residents of Kenilworth lived in stately homes on winding, tree-lined streets. A private security force patrolled streets day and night.

The seventeen-room Percy home, partly enclosed by a stockade-type fence and partly by a stone wall, was built on three acres of land on the shore of Lake Michigan. With its thick wooden support beams, heavy hinged doors, and windows with leaded panes, it looked like an English country home. It had a private beach and its own tennis courts. Huge trees and thick shrubbery surrounded the house.

A few days after the murder, Chief Robert M. Daley of the Kenilworth police declared, "I think this crime is going to be solved, and we are going to do it by legwork and perseverance." Chief Daley was wrong. While he and his associates did work diligently, with assistance from other communities, the state, and the FBI, no one has ever been prosecuted for the crime. And officials admit it is not likely that anyone ever will be.

The tragedy of Valerie's death struck the Percy family in the midst of Mr. Percy's race for a seat in the U.S. Senate. Earlier in the year, Mr. Percy had made up his mind to give up his successful business for the venture into politics and he resigned as chairman of the board of directors of the multimillion-dollar Bell & Howell Corporation.

Mr. Percy's election bid was looked upon as yet another challenge for the one-time "boy wonder" who had gone on to achieve spectacular success. At the age of five, he was already selling magazine subscriptions. By the time he was eight, young Charles had several hundred dollars in the bank and an award for selling more magazine subscriptions than any other boy in the Chicago area.

While attending high school, Charles held three jobs at the same time — janitor, office boy, and newspaper carrier.

As a student at the University of Chicago, Percy operated a business that sold food, fuel, bed linens, and furniture to fraternity houses and other university residences. The business had a gross income of $150,000 a year. The university president described Percy as "the richest kid who ever worked his way through college."

In 1943, Percy married. He and his wife became the parents of twin girls, Valerie and Sharon, and a son, Roger. Mrs. Percy died during an operation when Valerie was five. Mr. Percy remarried in 1950.

Valerie inherited much of her father's determination and vigor. After graduating from Cornell, she plunged into her father's campaign. Her chief responsibility was to work with young volunteers, but she often accompanied her father on the campaign trail. "I don't have a [political] machine," Mr. Percy often said, "so I depend on Val to get the volunteers and workers."

The day before she died, a Saturday, Valerie spent at her father's campaign headquarters in Chicago, arriving at about nine A.M. by subway.

"Val always took the subway so she wouldn't tie up the family cars," a friend noted. The first thing she did that morning was join a group of volunteers in addressing envelopes.

That evening, Valerie entertained two friends who were also campaign workers, James Mann and Tully Friedman, at a quiet dinner party at the Percy home. Mann and Friedman had been working with Valerie, helping her in the organization of youth activities. The two young men left the Percy home around ten o'clock.

A couple of hours after Mann and Friedman left, Valerie's twin sister, Sharon, who had graduated from Stanford University that spring, returned home from a date. She found Valerie in bed watching television, and they chatted for a short time.

At around twelve-thirty A.M., Valerie's father arrived home after having delivered a campaign speech in Chicago. He watched television briefly, then went to bed in the room he shared with his wife down the hall from Valerie's room.

The Percy home was then quiet until around five A.M., when Mrs. Percy was awakened by moans from Valerie's bedroom. She got up to investigate. Upon entering the bedroom, she was horrified to see a stranger standing over her daughter's bed, shining a light on her body.

When the man saw Mrs. Percy, he wheeled and flashed the light at her eyes, temporarily blinding her. Mrs. Percy screamed and ran back to the master bedroom. The intruder fled. Mrs. Percy pressed a button that set off a loud rooftop siren.

By this time, Mr. Percy was awake. He and his wife went back to Valerie's room. Turning on the light, they saw her lying on the blood-soaked bed. Mrs. Percy tried to talk to her, but got no response. She did detect a faint heartbeat, however.

Meantime, Mr. Percy telephoned a doctor who lived nearby. When the doctor arrived, he found Valerie dead.

Kenilworth police, with help from the state police and police from nearby communities, began at once to try to solve the murder. They used metal detectors to search the grounds of the Percy home, their hope being to find the knife and blunt instrument that had been used in the attack. Vacuum cleaners were brought in to search the beach sand. Scuba divers probed the lake bottom near the Percy home. Nothing was found that could definitely be linked to the attack.

Neighbors, friends, members of Percy's staff, and his political associates were questioned, as were former dates of Valerie's. James Mann and Tully Friedman, the two friends of Valerie's who had had dinner with her on Saturday evening, were brought in. Police also questioned Frederick Millington, a houseman from England whom the Percys had recently hired. Millington had been sleeping in his quarters above the garage at the time the attack occurred. Neither Millington nor anyone else could shed any light upon the crime.

Other detectives lifted fingerprints from table tops, staircase handrails, doors, and windows in the Percy home. The bedclothes from Valerie's room and the nightgown she had been wearing were checked for fibers, hair, or other clues. A diary that Valerie had kept as a teenager was examined by the police. All telephones calls she had made during the week before her death were investigated.

It didn't take police long to figure out what had happened. They came to the conclusion that Valerie's attacker had entered the house from the beach because of footprints they found there. The footprints led from the shore to winding steps leading up to the lawn. From there, it was only a short walk across the patio to the music room at the northeast side of the house. There the intruder gained entry.

He first cut a small opening in the screen that covered the music room door. Using a glass cutter, he then cut through one of the door's glass panels. With the glass gone, it was a simple matter to reach through and unlock the door.

The intruder was apparently familiar with the layout of the house, for he made his way through the hallways and rooms quickly and quietly. He slipped through the music room and the spacious living room and then climbed a circular stairway leading to the second floor. At the top of the stairs, he turned down the hallway leading to Valerie's bedroom. To reach it, he had to pass Sharon's bedroom and the bedroom of the girls' half brother, Mark, eleven, who happened to be away on a camping trip.

The master bedroom, where Valerie's step-mother and father were sleeping, was at the other end of the hallway. A half sister, Gail, ten, was also sleeping in a second-floor bedroom. Another brother, Roger, nineteen, was away at college in California.

Robbery was ruled out as a possible motive. Valerie's wallet, which contained sixty dollars, and jewelry on top of her dresser were not touched. There was no evidence of anything else in the house having been disturbed.

Police noted that the Percy watchdog, a Labrador retriever, had failed to bark when the intruder broke into the house. The dog was kept in a passageway between the garage and the house, a passageway that was located at the end of the house opposite the music room. For that reason, the dog may not have been able to hear the attacker as he cut through the screen and glass of the music room door. But police examined the dog to determine whether it had been drugged.

Four days after the slaying, Mrs. Percy described for the police the man she had seen standing over Valerie's bed. "He shined a flashlight on her body," Mrs. Percy said. In that instant, Mrs. Percy caught a glimpse of the killer. The man was about 5 feet 8 in height and weighed 160 or 165 pounds.

Mrs. Percy's description of the killer did not help very much; it could have fit any number of men. Nor did the search for clues provide anything worthwhile. After a week of work, police had to admit they had no idea who killed Valerie Percy. They did not even know the reason she was murdered.

With his daughter's death, Mr. Percy suspended his campaign for the Senate. His Democratic opponent, Senator Paul Douglas, out of sympathy for the Percy family, stopped campaigning, too. Not until mid-October, a month after the tragedy, did the two candidates resume.

When Mr. Percy won the election, some political observers said it was because many people had voted for him because they felt sorry for the family. But political observers noted that Percy had pulled ahead in the polls during the summer and maintained that lead until election day.

The investigation into Valerie's death continued without providing any answers. Days melted into weeks, weeks into months, and still the police had no solution.

Senator Percy offered $50,000 in reward money for information leading to the conviction of the killer. That led to more suspects being named and more leads, but not to the case being solved. Over the years, some 14,000 people were questioned, and more than 1,300 leads were followed up.

Police eventually got nineteen confessions in the case — all of them hoaxes. In October 1966, a young man in Tucson, Arizona, confessed to the murder, but later denied having taken part in the crime. In 1971, police in South Yarmouth, Massachusetts, said a twenty-four-year-old man had admitted to the Percy killing, along with seventeen other murders. But his confession proved to be a fake.

Another confession came from a twenty-seven-year-old man in Miami. He claimed not only to have killed Valerie, but also President John F. Kennedy, who was assassinated in 1963, Senator Robert F. Kennedy, and civil rights leader Martin Luther King, Jr. Kennedy and King were shot in 1966. Police did not put much belief in that confession.

The Percy case took a curious turn in 1973 when reporter Art Petacque of the *Chicago Sun-Times* obtained a revealing statement from fifty-eight-year-old Leo Rugendorf, a former member of the Mafia. Rugendorf, who was near death from heart disease, had once supervised a gang of cat burglars who had robbed the homes of wealthy people. Rugendorf named two of his former burglars, Francis Hohimer and Frederick Malchow, as being involved in Valerie Percy's death.

At the time, Hohimer was serving a thirty-year sentence for armed robbery. Malchow had plunged to his death from a railroad bridge in 1967 after escaping from a Pennsylvania prison.

According to Petacque, Rugendorf said Hohimer had admitted playing a role in the murder crime. "They'll get me for the Valerie Percy murder," Hohimer had said. "The girl woke up, and I hit her on top of the head with a pistol."

Petacque also spoke to Hohimer's younger brother. The brother said that Frank was "real nervous and uptight" the day after the murder. He added that his brother had told him he "had to 'off' the girl."

But when questioned by Petacque and other investigators, Frank Hohimer denied being in the Percy home and killing Valerie. Instead, he named Malchow, his partner, as the killer, saying that on the morning of the crime, Malchow had to come to his apartment in blood-stained clothes.

In 1975, Hohimer wrote a book about his criminal past, titled *The Home Invaders*. In the book, Hohimer admits to a number of burglaries, including the robbery of Elvis Presley's mansion in Memphis. But he continued to deny any part in Valerie Percy's murder.

Since there was no physical evidence to link Hohimer to the murder, officials could not arrest and prosecute him. Nor was there any evidence to indicate that the deceased Malchow was guilty. The offer of $50,000 in reward money has been withdrawn. The murder of Valerie Percy remains unsolved.

The Dingo Murder Case

It was almost eight o'clock on a warm August evening in 1980 near Ayers Rock, a massive, dome-shaped landmark that rises out of the flat plains of Australia's remote Northern Territory. Under the clear, moonless sky, Michael and Lindy Chamberlain joined their fellow campers in preparing supper around the outdoor fireplaces.

The Chamberlains' younger son, Reagan, four, was already asleep in the tent. The older boy, Aidan, seven, armed with a flashlight, chased a mouse under a picnic table.

Lindy rocked nine-week-old Azaria, whom the family called Bubby, in her arms. When the baby had fallen asleep, Lindy carried her back to the tent and tucked her into her carrycot.

Back at the barbecue, Lindy opened a can of beans and began heating them for Aidan. It was Aidan who asked, "Is that Bubby crying?" Michael Chamberlain said he heard it, too.

Lindy dashed back to the tent to check on her infant daughter. She would later testify in court what she saw: The carrycot was empty, and the bedclothes scattered about. A dingo — an Australian wolflike, wild dog — was emerging from the tent, its head low, shaking something vigorously.

Then it dawned on Lindy. "My God!" she shrieked. "The dingo's got my baby!"

Within minutes of Lindy's cry, campers pulled on boots and jackets, grabbed flashlights and lanterns, and began searching the underbrush near the campgrounds. They found nothing.

The next day, they were joined by volunteers from motels and other campgrounds in the area. Native trackers were also called upon. But there was no sign of Azaria.

Local police suspected that Azaria was already dead. Lindy accepted that fact, too, although searchers had not yet given up hope.

Azaria's disappearance quickly became a nationwide sensation. Newspapers and television reporters began to arrive at Ayers Rock and bombard the Chamberlains with questions. BABY STOLEN BY DINGO AT AYERS ROCK, one headline read.

Even after the Chamberlains had returned to their home in Mount Isa, Queensland, several hundred miles to the east, the story would not die. Michael Chamberlain noticed that some people asked questions in a suspicious way, as if they felt Lindy and he were trying to hide something.

The Chamberlains also had to deal with the fact that the dingo is rather popular in Australia. Most people believe it has a gentle nature. There was widespread doubt as to whether the animal could carry off a baby from a campground where there were so many people around. T-shirts with the slogan THE DINGO IS INNOCENT began to be sold.

This may help to explain why the Chamberlains, instead of receiving sympathy after the tragedy they suffered, often had to cope with unfriendly people.

Eight days after Azaria's disappearance, a tourist found her clothing not far from Ayers Rock. But there was no sign of the child.

People then began asking how a dingo could have removed Azaria's clothes. The discovery of the clothing, which, according to one report, were found folded in a neat pile, made people doubt Lindy's story even more.

An official investigation was unable to find enough evidence to try Lindy for murder. But those who believed she was not telling the truth would not rest. A second investigation was ordered.

James Cameron, a British expert on evidence used in legal proceedings, testified he had conducted tests on Azaria's jumpsuit and had come to the conclusion that cuts on the jumpsuit collar were made by a pair of scissors, not by dingo teeth. Cameron also said that tests he had conducted with ultraviolet light revealed a blood-stained handprint on the jumpsuit. The print was too small to be a man's hand and too big to be a small child's. The finger of guilt pointed at Lindy.

To make matters worse, Joy Kuhl, an Australian biologist, testified that stains that had been found on the Chamberlains' car and on a pair of scissors they owned were blood stains, and the blood was from a child under ten years of age.

In September 1982, Lindy Chamberlain was brought into court and put on trial for murder. Seven months pregnant at the time, Lindy sat stone-faced while she listened to the prosecution charge that she had cut Azaria's throat in the family car and later buried the child's body near Ayer's Rock. "It's not true!" Lindy cried out as the prosecutor presented the case against her.

The police questioned Lindy about the hours following Azaria's disappearance. The Chamberlains had remained at the campsite, waiting for news from the police or the searchers.

"Mrs. Chamberlain," said the prosecutor, "is it not the case that your husband declined to search actively on that Sunday night because he knew that the baby was dead, and he knew that you had killed her?"

"No, definitely not," Lindy said.

"And is that not why you declined to actively search?

"I suggest," the prosecutor continued, "that the reason you and your husband stayed near the car while people were searching was, for some portion of the night at least, the child's body was in the car."

"Definitely not."

"You invented the story of the dingo removing the child from the tent."

"I definitely did not invent that story. It's the truth."

From the prosecution's standpoint, the case lacked one very important element — a motive. Why would Lindy Chamberlain, the mother of a loving family, have murdered her baby?

Although the prosecution was not able to answer that question, the jury pronounced Lindy guilty of murder. "There is only one sentence I can pass upon you," the judge told her, "hard labor for life."

Lindy stared straight ahead, saying nothing. She was taken away to Berrimah Prison in Darwin.

In prison, events continued to go against her. When she gave birth to a daughter, Kahlia, in jail, the baby was promptly taken from her. She later was set free for five months when her sentence was being appealed, but she was imprisoned again when the appeal was denied.

She spent her days in prison working as a cleaner and helping out in the kitchen. In her spare time, she made clothes for Kahlia and leather belts for the boys. On the wall of her cell, she taped a sign that announced: TOUGH TIMES DON'T LAST.

Meanwhile, Lindy's supporters were working on her behalf. The "Save Lindy" campaign in Melbourne and the "Chamberlain Innocence Committee" in Sydney collected more than 130,000 signatures from people who demanded a new trial.

Thirty-one scientists signed an open letter protesting the conclusions that had been drawn from Joy Kuhl's evidence. A psychologist who examined Lindy in prison appeared on television to state that she seemed incapable of criminal behavior.

Berrimah Prison could scarcely handle the bagloads of mail that arrived for Lindy from her supporters. She answered those who wrote with a weekly newsletter. "God and I are doing O.K.," said one.

During her trial and even before, Lindy had insisted that not all of Azaria's clothing had been found. A little jacket was missing, she said. The prosecution had said she was lying, that she made up the story of the jacket in an effort to explain why no saliva from the dingo had been found on Azaria's other clothing.

Then in February 1986, searchers looking for the body of a British tourist who had fallen from Ayers Rock found Azaria's jacket. The amazing find gave new support to Lindy's account of how Azaria had disappeared. "I knew it would be realized that a mistake had been made," Lindy said.

Later that year, Lindy heard more good news. A Royal Commission of Inquiry announced that what was said to have been blood on the car dashboard was not blood at all but probably old food or a car repair chemical.

In September 1988, a court in Darwin overturned Lindy's conviction and declared her to be innocent of all charges. The long ordeal was over at last.

The Dingo murder case has made Lindy Chamberlain known throughout the world. At least six books have been written about Azaria's disappearance. Three television documentaries have been produced. In 1988, a feature film based on the case, titled *A Cry in the Dark,* was released. Meryl Streep played the role of Lindy Chamberlain.

The public's interest in the case continues. While most people agree that Lindy is innocent, there are some who still feel Lindy Chamberlain is a murderer. They question how a dingo, an animal rarely known to attack humans, could have carried off a nine-pound baby, leaving no trace.

Lindy herself realizes the questions will never end. "Some people will die believing we did it," she says.

Collision in the Sky

Around noontime on the last day of June in 1956, Fred Riley, driving his Ford pickup along a stretch of Arizona highway near the Grand Canyon, looked through his windshield at two big planes in the sky about ten miles ahead of him. For a moment, he took his eyes off the aircraft. When he looked back, the two shapes had merged into one. Then one of the planes broke apart from the other and plunged straight down. The aircraft that remained glided for a bit, then it, too, fell from the sky.

Riley couldn't believe what he had seen. He thought it might be some visual trick caused by the shimmering heat rising from the bleak desert.

A quiet man, Riley didn't tell anyone what he had witnessed. He was afraid of being laughed at. But that day Fred Riley was the only genuine eyewitness to the collision of two four-engine passenger planes and what was, at the time, the worst disaster in the history of commercial aviation in the United States.

The nightmarish crash brought death to 128 people and led to an investigation that lasted for almost a year. While investigators were able to re-create exactly what happened in the sky that day, they were never able to say exactly why it happened.

Why hadn't the pilots seen one another and taken evasive action? Several different answers to that question were suggested. The right one is anybody's guess.

Only three minutes apart, the two huge passenger planes had lifted into the hazy sky from Los Angeles International Airport on the morning of June 30. Both aircraft were in first-class operating condition. Their pilots, both men in their forties, were skilled and experienced. Each had flown this route dozens of times.

First went TWA's Flight 2, a silvery Super Constellation. It carried sixty-four passengers and a crew of six. Kansas City was scheduled as its first stop.

Behind the TWA flight came United Air Lines Flight 718, a DC-7 with fifty-three passengers and a crew of five. It was bound for Chicago and New York.

Both pilots had filed flight plans that called for them to depart from the standard airways after leaving Los Angeles. There was nothing out of the ordinary about this.

The airways, which are invisible but clearly defined aerial highways that are carefully monitored by air traffic controllers, sometimes mandated that pilots take roundabout routes. As a result, the airways were often bypassed by pilots who were seeking shortcuts or attempting to avoid strong headwinds.

If the TWA flight had stayed on airways, it would have had to detour to the south, flying to Kansas City by way of Albuquerque, New Mexico. The Chicago-bound United Air Lines flight would have had to swing north over Salt Lake City, Utah.

Instead, both pilots decided to fly direct to their destinations. But this decision changed the rules that governed the conduct of each flight. Once off the airways, the pilots would be fully responsible for avoiding other aircraft. There would be no assistance from air traffic controllers. It would be a case of "see and be seen."

As the two aircraft left Los Angeles airspace, the TWA flight was cleared to cruise at 19,000 feet. The United plane was assigned a cruising altitude of 21,000 feet.

Twenty minutes out of Los Angeles, the TWA flight asked for permission to change altitude to 21,000 feet. It is likely that Captain Jack Gandy was seeking to avoid bad weather, or turbulent air, or both. But the Los Angeles air traffic controller denied Gandy's request because there was too much traffic; the skies were relatively crowded.

Gandy then asked permission to fly "1,000 on top," that is, to fly a thousand feet over the cloud cover. The air traffic controller granted permission for this change but cautioned Gandy and the other crew members that United 718 was cruising at 21,000 feet in the same area.

Pilot Gandy acknowledged the message. Shortly after, he checked in over Daggett, California.

Nothing was heard from either plane for the next half hour. Then came another routine check-in call from the TWA plane. "Over Lake Mojave at 10:55," the message said, "one thousand on top at twenty-one thousand, estimating Painted Desert, eleven-thirty-one."

Three minutes later, Captain Robert Shirley, piloting the United Air Lines flight, was heard from. "Over Needles at 10:58," he said, "twenty-one thousand, estimating Painted Desert at 'thirty-one."

The messages, which indicated the two planes were to arrive at Painted Desert at the same time at the same altitude, would seem to have indicated a possible disaster. But none of the air traffic controllers who heard the messages got excited. That's because to them, "Painted Desert" was not a city or town, not some identifiable spot on a map. Painted Desert was a line of position, an imaginary line that connected two small ground stations, one in Utah, the other in Arizona, about 175 miles apart. To air traffic controllers, there was nothing at all ominous in the two messages. They simply indicated the two planes would be crossing that very long line at the same time. No problem.

The radios became silent again. Then at about 11:28 A.M., air traffic control heard a message that began, "Salt Lake from United 718 . . ." The rest was smothered by static. Those who heard the message included the pilot of another United Flight. He, along with the air traffic controllers, believed United 718 was having radio trouble. Nothing more was heard from the flight.

When United Flight 718 failed to check in over the Painted Desert Line, United Airlines tried calling Pilot Shirley. Unable to reach him, they asked other airlines for word on the plane. It was then they learned that TWA was unable to establish contact with its Flight 2. Shortly after, a full emergency was declared and the search began.

Early that evening, Palen Hudgin, who operated scenic flights for tourists over the magnificent gorges of the Grand Canyon, was the first to spot the wreckage. "At 12:15 P.M.," he later said, "I saw light smoke down inside the canyon and thought little about it. Later that evening I heard over the radio that two planes were missing, so I went back just before dark and flew over the smoke again and saw a wreck." Hudgin later spotted the shattered pieces of the TWA Constellation, which he was able to identify by markings on the tail surfaces.

The next day, on another flight, Hudgin found the remains of the United DC-7. It was less than a mile north from where the TWA wreckage lay.

Because of the rugged terrain, the wreck sites were virtually unreachable by foot or on horseback. A helicopter managed a landing on the day after the crash. The three-man helicopter crew sifted through the twisted wreckage. Bodies were burned and battered beyond recognition. There were no survivors.

Investigators recovered not only the bodies of the crash victims, but also bits and pieces of twisted metal that might contain clues. The evidence was tagged and shipped to the headquarters of the Civil Aeronautics Board (CAB) in Washington, D.C. There scientists and accident investigation specialists began a long and careful study of the battered metal.

Had the two planes actually collided in the skies over the Grand Canyon? And if they had struck, why had they? What had gone wrong?

These were the chief questions that the airlines, government agencies, and pilot organizations sought to answer in the months that followed the accident.

Several crumpled pieces of aluminum found a good distance from the main wreckage provided vital information. One of these pieces was the left wing panel of the United plane. The other was the left outer tailfin from the triple tail of the TWA Constellation.

Both pieces were heavily damaged. But what was significant was that the areas of damage fit together like two pieces in a jigsaw puzzle. The left wingtip of the United plane had slashed into the TWA plane's tail.

Not far away, investigators discovered another fragment of the United plane's left wingtip. Clinging to it was a piece of fabric from the ceiling of the TWA Constellation.

There was more. Propeller cuts were found in a chunk of metal from the belly section of the TWA plane. In one of these gashes, investigators found paint particles that were traced to a propeller from the United DC-7.

This evidence not only confirmed that the two aircraft had collided in midair, it also enabled investigators to reconstruct exactly how the accident had taken place. The TWA plane was traveling at a slightly slower rate of speed than the United DC-7, which came upon the Constellation from above and behind. The United plane knifed downward across the rear section of the Constellation, its left wing ripping off the Constellation's tail.

As part of the investigation, the CAB had a research laboratory analyze a tape recording of the last radio message from the United flight. Experts played it over and over for days. They finally determined there were two voices on the tape. One was that of the copilot of the DC-7, Robert W. Harms. He spoke in desperate tones, saying, "Salt Lake City from United 718 . . . ah . . . we're going *in*!"

The other voice, although it could not be identified, was even more ominous. It said, *"Pull up! Pull up!"*

The tailless Constellation was believed to have nosed downward and fallen like a stone. A number of coats and pillows from the plane were found scattered near the canyon rim. Investigators concluded they had been sucked out of the broken fuselage as the plane plummeted down. From the position of the wreckage, it was determined the aircraft was upside down when it struck the ground.

The United plane lingered in the air for several more seconds. With the outer third of its left wing destroyed, the aircraft turned and twisted crazily, traveling another mile or so, pitching downward as it went. One can only imagine what those last terrifying seconds must have been like for the passengers and crew. Death was certain — and everyone knew it.

Now there could be no doubt that the planes had met in the sky. The reason they had collided, concluded the CAB, "was that the pilots did not see each other in time."

That conclusion raised a question that cried out for an answer: Why didn't the pilots see one another? How was it possible for them to race toward their fatal meeting, each unaware of the other?

Several answers were suggested by the CAB in its accident investigation report, issued some ten months after the crash. One or several could have played a role.

Cockpit visibility — or lack of it — was possibly a factor, said the CAB. The way in which the cockpits were constructed created some blind areas. One study of cockpit visibility that covered six different passenger planes revealed that the best of them, the DC-3 of the 1930s and 1940s, allowed a pilot to see only 21.5 percent of his normal field of vision. The Lockheed Constellation was rated at 17.2 percent. The DC-7, the United plane, had the lowest score of all — 13.8 percent.

"The fact is," said TWA Captain John Carroll, a veteran pilot, "a pilot often finds it almost impossible to see another airplane, even when it's right beside him — particularly when its paint job camouflages it against the ground or sky, or when sun glare is bad, as it often is at high altitudes."

Investigators established there were thunderstorms in the area at the time of the accident. Towering white thunderhead clouds could have hampered visibility. These clouds could possibly have been positioned between the two aircraft at a critical moment.

It could also have been, said investigators, that the pilots and other crew members did not see each other simply because they were not looking. They might have instead been involved with standard cockpit duties. These included flying the aircraft, operating the radios, completing checklists, checking charts for radio frequencies or headings, maintaining logs, and recording flight-time data.

Investigators also suggested that the flight crews might not have been looking because of "preoccupation with matters unrelated to cockpit duties . . ." In specific terms, the CAB report said that at the time of the crash, the pilots may have been attempting to provide passengers with a more scenic view of the Grand Canyon area. Sightseeing was known to have taken place on commercial flights, with pilots banking or circling so passengers could get a better view of the awesome gorges below.

"The principal reason why pilots don't do more looking out of the cockpit is partly psychological," one airline captain said at the time of the crash. "We have been so indoctrinated in instrument flying practices and it has become so necessary to fly our modern transports with almost constant help from instruments that we have difficulty in constantly shifting our attention from the instrument panel to the outside.

"We might also say," he added, "we have been taught to do everything but look out."

Air traffic control procedures in effect at the time did not help matters. When the TWA plane climbed to 21,000 feet, the same altitude at which the United plane was flying, that information was never passed on to the United flight crew. There was no requirement for doing so. Off the airways, which was uncontrolled airspace, either flight was free to fly any route or altitude it pleased. "Dangerous freedom," is what one critic called the system.

While there were many theories, investigators could give no specific reason why the collision had taken place. "It is not possible to determine why the pilots did not see each other . . ." declared the official accident investigation report issued by the

CAB. One or a combination of factors were probably involved.

It was generally agreed, however, that the nation's air traffic control system failed that day. Drastic improvements were needed.

New regulations were adopted that cut back on the freedom that had existed. Limitations were put on the use of "1,000 on top," which had figured in the disaster.

"Positive separation" became the order of the day. Each plane flying above a certain altitude was given its own chunk of airspace by traffic controllers. All other planes were forbidden to enter it.

New electronic devices were put into use. The transponder was one. It beeps a warning when two planes are on a collision course, then instructs the pilots by means of arrows on the instrument panel which way to turn to avoid trouble. Another version automatically adjusts each plane's flight plan to avoid collision.

Commercial airliners that were developed in the years that followed, such as the Douglas DC-8 and the Boeing 707, provided somewhat better cockpit visibility. Nevertheless, the pilot still has huge blind spots behind and below him.

While there have been vast improvements in air traffic control in the decades since the Grand Canyon collision, collisions and near misses are still a serious problem. In 1986, an Aeromexico DC-9 and a Piper PA28 met in the sky over Cerritos, California. Eighty-two people died.

Hundreds of passengers have been involved in near collisions in recent years. In August 1987, over Santa Monica, California, an American Airlines jet with seventy-eight passengers aboard, had to roll nearly on its side and dive to miss a small aircraft as it sought to land at Los Angeles International Airport.

A few days later, none other than President Ronald Reagan experienced a near collision. As Reagan's helicopter was preparing to land at the presidential ranch in Santa Barbara, California, a small Piper Archer private plane entered the security zone and passed 150 feet below the president's craft. Reagan was astonished the plane had come so close.

One problem today is that passenger airliners are routed through the same airspace as much smaller, noncommercial aircraft. Many small, private planes lack transponders that would make their presence known to radarscopes manned by traffic controllers. The pilots of these planes are using their eyes to keep themselves clear of commercial airlines (and, on occasion, presidential helicopters).

Critics say that the nation's air traffic control system did not keep pace with the growth in air travel during the 1980s. More controllers are needed, it's said. All planes should be equipped with collision-warning devices, not just commercial aircraft.

Almost forty years ago, the consequences of fate brought TWA 2 and United Airlines 718 together over the Grand Canyon, an accident that triggered major advances in air traffic control procedures. It would be sad if it took another major tragedy to convince people that more improvements are now needed.

Zodiac

In the late 1970s and early 1980s, law enforcement officials in the United States and Canada became aware that there had been a sharp increase in murder cases involving one murderer and several victims. Often no motive could be found in these crimes, no obvious link between killer and victims.

Law enforcement officials came to describe such crimes as "serial murders." Sadly, their number is still on the rise.

One of the first and most publicized serial murder cases began in California in 1968 and continued for the next several years. The killer was known as "Zodiac" because the letters and cryptograms he sent to newspapers contained drawings representing astrological signs.

No one knows for certain how many people fell victim to Zodiac. Estimates range from five to forty.

Millions of dollars were spent investigating the crimes. A dozen or so law enforcement agencies were involved. Thousands of witnesses were questioned. While Zodiac was actually seen on a number of occasions, there was no agreement as to what he actually looked like. The identity of Zodiac is as much a mystery today as it was more than twenty years ago when the first killings began.

The first of Zodiac's victims were a pair of Vallejo, California, teenagers — David Faraday and Betty Lou Jensen — who were out on their first date together. On the evening of December 20, 1968, they had parked their 1961 Rambler station wagon near a pump house above the Lake Herman Reservoir.

Police had warned couples of the danger of parking in such an isolated area. But the spot was popular with kids because they could see the headlights of other cars as they came around the curve in the road.

At around eleven o'clock that night, Homer Your and his wife, Peggy, drove out to Lake Herman Road. Mr. Your wanted to check out the water pipes his company had been installing near the pump house. When they passed the Rambler station wagon, the Yours saw David sitting in the driver's seat. Betty Lou was leaning against his shoulder.

After looking over the construction site, the Yours turned around and drove back past the station wagon again. David and Betty Lou were still sitting in the same position.

Around 11:15, Mrs. Stella Borges left her ranch on Lake Herman to pick up her thirteen-year-old son who had gone to a movie in the town of Benicia. As Mrs. Borges turned the corner of the road near where David had parked, her car's headlights picked up a very different scene. What Mrs. Borges saw shocked and horrified her.

The right front door of the Rambler was open, and Mrs. Borges thought the young man had fallen out of the car. He was lying on his back and breathing in loud gasps. Then she saw the bullet wound near his left ear and the large pool of blood forming about his head.

Beyond the car, Mrs. Borges saw Betty Lou's body. She had been shot several times in the back, obviously while trying to flee.

Mrs. Borges sped from the scene to look for help. When she spotted a police car, she honked and blinked her lights.

Both teenagers were dead when the police arrived at the pump house. There was no apparent motive for the killings. David's wallet had not been stolen. Betty Lou lay where she had fallen, her clothing undisturbed.

With so few clues to go on, the police were frustrated. The investigation soon ground to a halt. The two teenagers became statistics in California's roster of unsolved murders.

More than six months later, at 12:40 A.M. on July 5, 1969, a gruff-voiced man called the Vallejo police headquarters and said, "I want to report a double murder." He then told in detail where the bodies could be found and added, "They are shot with a 9-mm Luger. I also killed those kids last year. Good-bye."

Actually, the scene of the attack had already been discovered. And just minutes before the call was made, Darlene Ferrin, a twenty-two-year-old waitress at Terry's Restaurant in Vallejo, had been brought to the hospital, dead. The other victim, Michael Mageau, nineteen, was seriously wounded.

Later, Mike was able to tell police what had happened. He and Darlene were going to the movies together in her 1963 bronze Corvair. She was at the wheel; Mike sat next to her. From the time they set out, it seemed as if they were being trailed by a light-colored car. Darlene turned into the parking lot at the Blue Rock Springs Golf Course, which happened to be only a couple of miles from the site of the Faraday-Jensen murders less than seven months before.

They had been sitting in the darkness for only a moment when a car pulled up beside them. The driver was a heavyset man, Mike could tell.

"Do you know who it is?" Mike asked Darlene.

Her answer puzzled him. "Oh, never mind," she said. "Don't worry about it."

Almost immediately, the car pulled away. Mike breathed a sigh of relief. But five minutes later, it was back.

This time, a bright and powerful light was beamed at them from the other car. Then it started moving toward them. Mike thought it was the police. "Here come the cops," he said to Darlene.

"You'd better get your identification out."

Suddenly the light went out, and someone started shooting. Several bullets struck Darlene, and others entered Mike's neck, right arm, and left leg. The gunman walked back to his car and hurried away, his tires screeching. Witnesses nearby heard the shots and called police.

Mike had been able to see the face of the attacker. He described him as stocky, about five feet eight, and between twenty-six and thirty years old. He had curly, light brown hair.

Police believed the caller when he said he was the gunman in both crimes, even though the gun he used in the attack on Darlene and Michael was not the same as the one used in killing the teenagers in December. Police also came to the conclusion that the killer probably lived in or near Vallejo because he seemed so familiar with the area.

Four weeks after Darlene Ferrin's murder, the case took a bizarre twist when a newspaper in Vallejo and two in San Francisco received scrawled letters from the killer. All of the letters contained details of the crimes that were unknown to the general public, so the police had no doubt the signer was telling the truth when he proclaimed himself to be the gunman.

Each letter contained a torn sheet of paper bearing a strange-looking cipher or coded message. It was composed of a mix of letters of the English alphabet, Greek letters, astrological symbols, and others. One of the ciphers looked like this:

In the letters that accompanied the coded messages, the gunman instructed the newspapers to print the cipher "on the front page." If they failed to do so, the killer threatened to go on a rampage. The letters were signed with a symbol: a circle containing a cross inside it.

All three newspapers published the cipher. But they did not tell their readers of the murder threat because they did not want to frighten people.

The newspapers also asked the writer to provide more information as to his identity. He wrote to the papers again, providing more details about the attacks. This time the letters began: "This is Zodiac speaking . . ." It marked the first time he had used the name.

The cipher wasn't hard to crack, although the task was made more difficult because there were so many mistakes in spelling. The message began: "I like killing people because it's so much fun . . ." It went on to tell how the victims were destined to become the killer's slaves "for my afterlife." But it did not reveal his identity.

The killer struck again on Saturday, September 27, 1969. Two studens from Pacific Union College, twenty-year-old Bryan Hartnell and Cecelia Ann Shepard, who was twenty-two, went to the park near Lake Berryessa, east of Santa Rosa, for a picnic. They had just finished eating when a frightening figure advanced toward them out of a grove of trees.

He wore a hood that had slits for the eyes and mouth cut into the cloth. Sewn on the biblike front of the hood was a white cross inside a circle — Zodiac's sign. Strapped to his left side was a knife with a blade that was at least a foot long. In his right hand he carried a pistol.

At first it seemed to be no more than a robbery. The man asked for money and the car keys. "I want your car to go to Mexico," he said. Bryan handed over the money he had, apologizing because it was so small an amount, and the keys to his Volkswagen sports car.

Then the man ordered the two students to lie down on the ground. From beneath his jacket he produced several feet of plastic clothesline. "Tie the boy up," the man said to Cecelia. When she finished, the man tied her up.

Then the man announced, "I'm going to have to stab you people." And he did so, repeatedly. Bryan managed to survive the attack. But Cecelia did not.

A fisherman on the lake heard their screams and rowed to the headquarters of a park ranger, who raced to the scene. Soon after, the police arrived. They had learned of the attack from a gruff voice on the telephone telling them he wanted to report a double murder, and describing the location.

At Lake Berryessa, police found that the killer had written a message on the passenger door of Bryan's car with a felt-tipped pen, the same kind of writing instrument that had been used in all of Zodiac's letters. The message read:

> Vallejo
> 12-20-68
> 7-4-69
> Sept 27-69-6:30
> by knife

The dates listed were when the other attacks had taken place. Above the message, the killer had drawn the now familiar Zodiac symbol, a cross in a circle.

Just two weeks later, on the night of October 11, 1969, Zodiac struck a fourth time. The victim was Paul Lee Stine, a twenty-nine-year-old student who worked part-time as a cab driver.

Stine picked up a stocky man in the theater district of San Francisco. As he settled into the backseat, the man asked to be taken to an address in Presidio Heights, a residential section of the city.

About a quarter of an hour later, Stine's cab pulled up to the corner of Cherry and Washington

Streets, a block from his destination. A gunshot rang out.

What happened next was viewed by a group of teenagers who were having a party in a building across the street from where Stine's cab was parked. They watched as a man got out of the backseat and reached through the driver's window. There was the sound of tearing cloth and then the man wiping the car door and dashboard with a rag, as if to remove fingerprints. When he had finished, the man walked off into the night.

From the teenagers, the police were able to get a good description of the man. He was a white male with reddish or blond crew-cut hair. He was about five feet eight and around thirty years old. He wore glasses, a navy-blue or black jacket, and dark trousers.

A police artist prepared a sketch of the suspect. A copy was sent to every taxicab company in San Francisco. Police wanted cab drivers to be on guard, in case the gunman planned to repeat the attack.

Three days after the killing of Paul Stine, the *San Francisco Chronicle* received a letter from Zodiac. "I am the murderer of the taxi driver," the letter began. To prove the letter was actually from the killer, Zodiac enclosed a piece of the cab driver's blood-stained shirt.

The letter ended with a chilling threat. "School children make nice targets," said Zodiac. "I think I shall wipe out a school bus some morning. Just shoot out the front tire & then pick off the kiddies as they come bouncing out."

Police felt they had no choice but to release the contents of the letter to the public. Newspapers in northern California featured the story under big headlines. Television and radio stations blared the news night and day.

Near panic was the result. Thousands of parents decided to drive their children to school rather than permit them to ride school buses, even though they were provided with special police protection. In San Francisco, for example, police in unmarked cars trailed school buses as they made their morning and afternoon rounds.

In the Napa Valley, where Zodiac's first attacks had taken place, police declared a state of emergency. A heavily armed police officer was assigned to each school bus and instructed to take command of the vehicle should it come under attack. Pickup trucks from the forestry department and ranger stations at Lake Berryessa were ordered to follow the buses. Small aircraft from the Sheriff's Department and the Napa Aero Club patrolled the bus routes from overhead.

Each driver was given special instructions to follow should Zodiac, as he had announced, shoot holes in the front tire.

1. Continue driving on the flat tire. Turn on all lights. Sound the horn. Do not stop.

2. Tell the children to get below the level of the window and lie down on the floor.

3. Do not stop until arriving at a well-populated area. Then notify a local law enforcement agency.

Some observers accused Napa school officials of overreacting. This brought a heated response. "How can you overreact to such a threat?" one official asked. "We're worrying whether we've done enough. If a madman could get to President Kennedy [who had been assassinated some six years before], with all the protection he had, then it could happen in Napa, even with all we've done."

Thankfully, the killer never made any attempt to carry out an attack on a school bus. The murder of cabdriver Paul Stine was, in fact, the last killing blamed on the Zodiac by police.

But that was not the end of the case. On October 22, a husky-voiced man who claimed to be Zodiac telephoned the Oakland, California, police department. He said he would be willing to give himself up if he could be represented by a famous lawyer. He named the silver-haired Melvin Belli and F. Lee Bailey, who had once represented "The Boston Strangler." The caller said he would contact one of the lawyers if he appeared on a popular early-morning San Francisco television talk show hosted by Jim Dunbar.

The San Francisco police decided it was worth a try. They asked Melvin Belli, whose main office was in San Francisco, to cooperate and he agreed. Jim Dunbar promised to help, too. He asked his radio audience not to call in on the day of Belli's appearance, but to leave the lines open so Zodiac could get through.

On the agreed-upon day when the show went

on the air, it had a record audience. The program had been on for about a half an hour when a soft boyish voice came on the line. The caller identified himself as Zodiac. Belli asked the man to give him a name that was not quite so frightening. "Sam," the man said.

"Sam" hung up and then called back. He made repeated brief calls for almost two hours. Thirteen were heard on the air. Police theorized that "Sam" made very short calls because he believed a short call could not be successfully traced.

"Sam" talked about the murders he had committed and the terrible headaches he had suffered, ever since "I killed that kid last December [Betty Lou Jensen]." The caller's remarks were interrupted by groans of pain, which, he explained, "were the headaches speaking." Belli tried to persuade the caller to give himself up, but he refused.

He did, however, agree to meet Belli in front of a store in Daly City, just south of San Francisco. Belli showed up (along with the police), but the killer did not.

Three people who, at one time or another, had actually heard Zodiac speak — a police officer, a switchboard operator, and Bryan Hartnell, who had survived the stabbing at Lake Berryessa — listened to a tape recording of "Sam's" telephone conversation with Melvin Belli. They didn't think the voice sounded like Zodiac's.

And they were right. Eventually police determined that "Sam" was a patient in a state mental hospital. It was not possible that he was Zodiac.

Yet the real Zodiac was almost certainly aware of the television program arranged by the San Francisco police and the role that Belli had played in it, for late in December that year, Belli received what was surely a genuine letter from Zodiac. Enclosed with the letter was another scrap of Paul Stine's blood-stained shirt. In the letter, Zodiac claimed eight victims, and warned he would kill again.

There was a note of desperation in the letter. "I cannot reach out for help because this thing in me won't let me," Zodiac said. "I am finding it extremely difficult to hold myself in check and I am afraid I will lose control and take my ninth and possibly tenth victim.

"Please help me . . ."

In the months that followed, the police, area newspapers, and a number of well-known individuals received "Zodiac letters." While some looked to be genuine, there is no proof any of them were. They represented the work of hoaxers.

Psychologists studied the authentic Zodiac letters and other materials associated with the crimes. Some described Zodiac as a person with no importance, no influence, a nobody. With his murderous crimes, he had gained what he had always wanted — attention, public recognition, a kind of fame.

"He kills senselessly because he is deeply frustrated," wrote Dr. Laurence Freedman, "and he hates himself because he's an anonymous nonentity. When he is caught, he will turn out to be a mouse, a murderous mouse."

The San Francisco police believed Zodiac had been responsible for six murders. But Zodiac himself claimed to have murdered thirty-seven people.

Evidence that Zodiac's total may have been quite accurate came in 1975 from Don Striepke, sheriff of California's Sonoma County. Using a computer, Striepke analyzed the murder records of four Western states. He found similarities in approximately forty of them. Sheriff Striepke believed these forty murders were the work of one killer — Zodiac.

For the next fifteen years, nothing was heard of Zodiac. California police felt Zodiac was either dead or being held in a mental institution.

Then, in the spring of 1990, Zodiac suddenly blazed back into the headlines. This time New York City was the scene.

Early in March that year, Mario Orosco, fifty, a man who walked with a cane, was shot as he was returning to his home in the East New York section of Brooklyn from his job in Manhattan.

After shooting Orosco, the gunman waited until the end of the month until he struck again. On March 29, 1990, again in East New York, he shot and wounded thirty-four-year-old Germaine Montenesdro.

Both shootings were investigated by the police. But no link was established until notes believed to have been written by the gunman were received by the *New York Post* and the CBS television program *60 Minutes*. The letters, which contained information about the shootings only the attacker could have known, began with the words, "This is Zodiac . . ." The notes also contained drawings of Zodiac symbols inside a sphere. The drawings were done in felt-tip pen.

On May 31, Zodiac struck a third time, shooting Joseph Proce, seventy-eight, in the back. Proce was attacked not in Brooklyn, as the others had been, but in Woodlawn, Queens. Not long after the shooting, Proce died of his wounds.

At the scene of the shooting, police found a note near the body. "Zodiac — time to die," it said. Like the previous note, it contained drawings of astrological signs.

The gunman claimed a fourth victim late in June by shooting Larry Parham, thirty, a homeless man, in the chest as he slept on a bench in Central Park. A folded note was found underneath a rock on the bench. The note had astrological drawings identical to the previous notes. But to mark the fourth shooting, a fourth astrological sign had been added.

Police found a .38 caliber bullet lodged in the park bench where Parham had been sleeping. Police said the bullet matched another slug that was recovered after the third shooting. "This was the same gun and the same gunman," said a detective.

Throughout the summer of 1990, New York police kept alert for another attack. A special task force was organized to deal with the case. But the gunman never struck again.

In their efforts to trace the killer, New York police officials checked a theory that the gunman might be a copycat who followed the example of San Francisco's Zodiac killer. This theory was supported by Candice Skrapec, a psychologist and professor of criminology at the John Jay College of Criminal Justice in New York. According to Skrapec, the New York gunman seemed to pattern his crime wave on *Zodiac*, a bestselling book by Robert Graysmith published in 1986. "I feel more assured than ever," Skrapec told the *New York Post,* "that he has seen the book and read at least parts of it.

"It is still possibly a coincidence, but some of the wording in the note is very similar to the notes in the book." Skrapec pointed out that letters from both the San Francisco and New York gunman began: "This is Zodiac speaking."

While there were similarities in the two cases, police were convinced that the New York and San Francisco killers were not the same. The descriptions of what the gunmen looked like were different. The handwriting in the notes in San Francisco and those received in New York were different.

There was, however, one other glaring similarity in the two cases: No solution has been been found in either of them.